ALSO BY E. M. BRONER

FICTION

Journal/Nocturnal and Seven Stories

Her Mothers

A Weave of Women

Ghost Stories

DRAMA

Summer Is a Foreign Land

NONFICTION

The Lost Tradition: Mothers and Daughters in Literature
(with Cathy N. Davidson)

*The Telling: The Story of a Group of Jewish Women Who
Journey to Spirituality Through Community and Ceremony*

Mornings and Mourning: A Kaddish Journal

The Women's Haggadah (with Naomi Nimrod)

Bringing Home the Light: A Jewish Woman's Handbook of Rituals

THE RED SQUAD

THE RED

SQUAD

E. M. Broner

Pantheon Books
New York

BRONER
E.M.

Copyright © 2009 by Esther Broner
All rights reserved. Published in the United States by Pantheon Books, a division of Random House, Inc., New York, and in Canada by Random House of Canada Limited, Toronto.

Pantheon Books and colophon are registered trademarks of Random House, Inc.

Grateful acknowledgment is made to Hal Leonard Corporation for permission to reprint an excerpt from "What's Going On," words and music by Renaldo Benson, Alfred Cleveland, and Marvin Gaye, copyright © 1970 (Renewed 1998) by Jobete Music Co., Inc., MGIII Music, NMG Music, and FCG Music. All rights controlled and administered by EMI April Music Inc. on behalf of Jobete Music Co., Inc., MGIII Music, NMG Music, and FCG Music and EMI Blackwood Music Inc. on behalf of Stone Agate Music (a division of Jobete Music Co., Inc.). All rights reserved. International copyright secured. Reprinted by permission of Hal Leonard Corporation.

Library of Congress Cataloging-in-Publication Data
Broner, E. M.
The Red Squad / E. M. Broner.
p.   cm.
ISBN 978-0-307-37791-3
1. Women college teachers—Fiction. 2. Student movements—Fiction.
3. Nineteen sixties—Fiction. 4. Subversive activities—Fiction.
5. Undercover operations—Fiction. 6. Detroit (Mich.)—Fiction. I. Title.
PS3552.R64R43 2009
813'.54—dc22   2008042274

www.pantheonbooks.com

Printed in the United States of America

First Edition

2 4 6 8 9 7 5 3 1

Dedicated to:

Mary Gordon, a great writer and constant friend

and the memory of John Leonard, critic, who validated us early on
and gave heart to decades of writers

CHARACTERS *(some under surveillance)*

BULLPENNERS

Anka Pappas: Young instructor, the heifer in the Bullpen.

Kevin Kelly: Priest seeking formal release from the Church.

Farmer: Both his previous occupation and the pastoral theme for his dissertation.

Jack (Yaakov) Bernstein: PhDeified; loyal and paranoid.

Noble O'Dwyer: Poet, son of activist family.

Ron Ivory: African American, reluctantly given tenure in Victorian and Decadent Studies. Intimate of O'Dwyer's.

OTHERS

Elizabeth Farmer: Graduate student, dropped out of program to bear the Farmer children.

Chairman of the English Department: "Old Kraut"; bearer of ill tidings.

Mr. Berger: Student, source of fantastic tales.

Big Black Jerome: Student, employee of educational television.

Boiler Room (Thomas O'Connor), Fearless Phil (Philip Impelliteri), Florrie H.: Night composition students.

Assorted dissenters, picketers: Recorded by the Red Squad.

Ralph Sincere: Jailed White Panther.

Lobschultz: Parks Department; young fascist.

Little Mozart: Tormentor from the past.

The Spy: Known only to the Red Squad.

THE RED SQUAD

I have a small house, just my size. The problem is that what happens in one room echoes in the next. The television in the living room I hear in the library, even with the door closed. The radio in the kitchen speaks into the hallway and downstairs bedroom.

All sounds waft to the loft upstairs: the rockets' red glare, the bombs bursting in air.

I heard such sound effects forty years ago. The sound of explosives, the bombast of speech. This morning's mail brought me back to that other place in the most thrilling and terrible time of my youth.

I'm too old to be ducking the news. But the headlines continue to follow me.

NOW, 2000+: The Mysterious Package

The eight-and-a-half-by-eleven-inch envelope has been tossed negligently on the porch, where it freezes. It is a chilly day in early spring, March 10, whose date will echo in this history. When I pull the envelope loose from the icy cement I find that the contents have been pried from my own life.

The face of the white envelope is gaudy with instructions: stickers in the green family, blue-green and forest green, and an imperious red sticker, all having to do with postal matters: com-

pleting the return address on the back, acknowledgment of certi-
fied mail, return receipt requested.

I am free enough and old enough to choose when to encounter
weather. On this unpleasant day I stay indoors. No bell is rung.
No postal worker requests a signature or acknowledgment. I
become agitated. It is an old reaction to unsolicited mail, whose
contents can range from mildly intrusive to threatening.

Studying the envelope, I note, among other data, that the cost
of postage to sender is $3.21. Curiously, the name of sender is
omitted, yet an address is printed. I phone information (at the
cost of two dollars per inquiry), which gives me the phone number to the address. I am mechanically informed that the phone
line to 2800 Palm Building, downtown in my long-ago city with
its disappeared center, has been disconnected.

Then I open the envelope. Since I am warned not to reveal
these contents, I determine to reveal all. I have only one question
to ask. Sender. Tell me. If you please. Who was the spy who did
your bloody work for you?

THEN: The Sixties and Grading

I was assigned endless classes of Comp 101: Writing the Term
Paper. To prevent madness in the lower ranks, the department
allowed the instructors one class of choice in literature or creative
writing. In an inner-city university my students did not come
close to literature, but each had a hardscrabble tale to tell. So I, a
classicist in Greek, taught creative writing.

In those days I wasn't Helen of Troy, but I was of the same her-
itage, with a head full of curly black hair. I saw the films starring
the regal Irene Papas, with her fall of raven locks, and of Melina
Mercouri, a mischievous blonde.

My Mediterranean eyes were hidden behind the glare of glasses, prescribed after a semester of correcting the phonetic spelling of my students.

Hence the marginalia decorating their compositions, with "sp"; with "dis," not for "disrespect" but "discontinuity"; and "awk" for "awkward," that onomatopoeic abbreviation that crowed around their writings.

I was judgmental then, grading everyone and everything that came my way. In the university's gym, where I exercised before my morning class, I graded the person in front of me, unable to touch her toes or stretch her body to its full length (C minus). I graded people on the street for language and posture (also C minus). All "fucks" received an automatic failing.

I graded the cityscape, the slums that surrounded the campus (F as in "foul"). And I graded my office mates in the Bullpen of the English department, where I was the heifer.

I marked the priestly Kevin (A for height and brawn), the thorny Bernstein (B for loyalty but C for boring), the slight O'Dwyer (B for grace), and the skeletal, straight-haired Farmer, whose grade, as his persona, kept changing. Ron was our short, dark tribal leader for the time he was with us. He received an A for his rich baritone, elegance of dress, and patrician manner. He was the first of us commoners to be elevated out of the Pen.

Ron had his doctorate, Bernstein will defend his dissertation, and the rest of us were mere ABDs, stratification always present in the Bullpen.

Bernstein was the Bullpen put-down, his shrieking laugh bouncing off the walls of our cubicles.

"The Music department is having a fete," he said one day, exaggerating the French *fête*, "to be conducted by Dr. ABD, ably assisted by Master TIP. Who would go hear people in rehearsal to be themselves?"

Bernstein was nasty because he was closer to the finish line than we. Between Ph.D., ABD (All But Dissertation), and TIP (Thesis in Preparation), we nervously laughed. Not Farmer.

"Just tell me what's so funny," said Farmer, touchy about matters academic.

Inside the Bullpen, the atmosphere was heated, where desks yearned toward one another.

We were located next to the executive offices of the chairman, whose heavy tread we heard in the corridor. We Bullpenners were too lowly for his personal visits but received curt notes with his initials in our mailboxes, lying faceup. Anyone distributing notices to the department, pulling out noisy metal box after box, could have read of his displeasure.

We were aware that, on whatever door he knocked, he brought ill tidings: one experienced assistant professor, a gifted teacher with limited publication, would not be promoted; a well-published young woman was discernibly pregnant and that would interfere with her tenure.

The chairman was also the guardian of our proper behavior in those unsettling times. An instructor, whose hobby was building harpsichords from kits, was harshly reprimanded for dismissing his classes to hear an antiwar expert on Vietnam.

"This is an English department, not a war department!" we heard the chairman shout.

Mr. Bernstein called him the Kraut.

"That was a different war," I said.

"Same accent, same tread," said Mr. Bernstein, who holds a grudge forever. Germany was only the tail end of it. Bernstein was angry from the fifteenth and sixteenth centuries.

"I will never set foot on the soil of Castile, Aragon and Navarre, Sicily, or Portugal," he vowed, "nor where the arms of the Inquisition traveled to the New World, to Peru, Chile, Argentina, or Brazil."

Because everywhere you looked, explained Bernstein, countries drove the Jews into the sea, he traveled nowhere, except from New York to the Midwest and back east again. If it somehow worked out, his last voyage would be to the Middle East to settle in Zion.

"You're lucky you're Greek," he said.

A lucky Greek? I had luck in my breasts, too much luck in my hips, no luck in my waist.

My mother said my face made up for it: earth-brown eyes, serious brows, and "lips from a statue."

"If they resist you," my mother said, "they'll be sorry."

There was only one person I found irresistible, and he was not sorry, but resisted me.

Should I have informed Bernstein that there was no luck, only volatility, in Greek politics between the democrats and the colonels? But that would have lessened his own myths.

Bernstein, Jack, was always a last name to me, like Farmer and O'Dwyer. Only Kevin, our temporary priest, was called Kevin. He was addressed as "Father" too long, he explained, and longed for informality.

NOV. 2000+

The files in my envelope have various heads: "Confidential Report—Special Investigation Unit." "Detroit Police Department—Interoffice Memorandum." "Criminal Investigation Division." "Criminal Intelligence Bureau."

The repeat of "criminal" and handwritten comments in the margins frighten me even four decades later. "Red Squad" at the top of the first page. There they were in the sixties, crouched, aiming their weaponry at Reds. It reminded me of other Red Scare times: World War I and the deportation of a third of the Italian immigrant population; the McCarthy era, and the fleeing of moviemakers and poets. I felt like the billboards of Sherwin-Williams paint, an open can spilling red on the globe of the world. To the Red Squad, whoever they were, I am also colored in crimson.

Everything I think about the present and the past will be dictated by the enclosures of that envelope. Why was it sent to me? A reminder, a threat? I filed no Freedom of Information request. In fact, I have spent these years distancing myself from that time.

NOW AND THEN: The Outline

Outside of the Bullpen, I taught my students in that dreaded Comp 101 to write outlines.

Here is mine in regards to this odyssey:

The Bullpen
Frozen Contract
Laughter and Subversive Planning
Meetings
The Cast of Heroic and Villainous Characters
Partying on Down
False Arrest
Finking on Faculty
The Home of Mr. and Mrs. Farmer
Bullpenner Disappears
The Betrayal
War Testimony
Bullpenners Dispersed
The New War
Street Marches

Reunion of the Bullpenners
The Fates Spin, Measure, and Shear

Somewhere in the long list there had to be room for "Passion," for we were in our midtwenties, away from home, and full of longing.

NOW, 2000+

I lift the sheets from the envelope and look closely at the listing of names. As I name the accused out loud, their faces emerge like flash cards.

They are our younger selves but filled with idealistic purpose. Some have stayed within the classroom, emerging for the arrival of the annual Modern Language Association meeting in places like San Francisco, D.C., New Orleans, or NYC. Others have dropped from academic sighting, not serving on boards, no longer read in the scholarly journals. They've been content to go local, showing up in Georgia at the Southeast Modern Language Association or the Midwest MLA in Laredo, Kansas.

Some we lost: the amateur harpsichordist, the pregnant assistant professor. Recently, there was recognition of one of us, not of name but of face, on the front page of the national press.

But all of us were under suspicion.

THEN: The Frozen Contract

Ron Ivory, ironic surname, was the first Black instructor in the English department (his thesis: "The Influence of Color in the Victorian Novel"). He found the contract offering him tenure also frozen to the porch. He had previously been summoned by our chairman ("Nineteenth-Century English Writers in Davos, Switzerland"), who sat so icily behind his desk that Ron knew the chairman had been outvoted by the Tenure Committee.

Ron didn't belong in the Bullpen. He belonged in the offices of the other instructors who had completed their oral presentations and dissertations. Space was the problem in the more private offices, he was told.

An extra desk was shoved into our Pen, scraping against O'Dwyer's.

"I hope you don't mind," Ron apologized.

Soon, O'Dwyer didn't mind at all.

At first we were cautious, treating Ron either as royalty or native. Then we became casual and profane. Ron rolled with it. Until he rolled right out of there.

Why did Ron buy a gun? Was it the concealed or revealed racism? Was it his living in the heart of the city without family? (But none of us, except for the married Farmers, had family.) Or being of small stature? Or simply his ebony color?

To us, his former Bullpenners, Ron made light of (intentional pun) circumstances. We heard him in the Bullpen conversing in French with a graduate student from Lyons. Nearby, one of Ron's freshmen, waiting for remedial help, watched with amazement.

"Do you people speak French?" he asked Ron.

"You people" speak the language of diplomacy?

I inadvertently discovered Ron registering for a gun at Sears, Roebuck, where Guns abutted Household Appliances. He looked up at me from the form he was filling out and said nothing. It would turn out later that Ron would not be the only alarmed and, therefore, armed person in the English department.

Ron took the stiff contract and used it as leverage. He was the first and only one of us to leave the Bullpen with the revenge of being hired from an inner-city university by a prestigious eastern college.

Ron returned regularly for his friend O'Dwyer, as well as Detroit music and a royal visit to the Pen.

We got on, Ron and I.

"'Sugar Pie, Honey Bunch,'" he greeted me. He never said anything personal. Motown, the Four Tops, in this case, spoke for him.

"How's 'My Girl'?" he would ask, then sing, "'My girl, my girl, talkin' 'bout my girl.'" (Or Smokey Robinson for the Temptations.)

"How's 'My Guy'?" Ron asked O'Dwyer.

Looking at Kevin out of the corner of my eye, I sang, "'Nothing you can say could tear me away from my guy (my guy).'"

"'My Guy,' 'My Girl,'" said Farmer. "Maybe Smokey swung both ways."

We were surprised to hear from Farmer. We thought of him as bluegrass.

Farmer had never impressed Ron.

"Everybody listen. A Farmer is speaking," said Ron.

Farmer was skinny. You could see the shape of bony knees beneath his pants. His face had no cheeks and thin lips. But he was flexible, rhythmic in that skeletal frame.

Bernstein showed no interest in music or anything hopping and popping. With his long nose, wiry hair, and rounded shoulders, he was the Pen Yid.

Kevin, the physical opposite of Bernstein, swiveled his desk chair and smiled. Motown was new to him, and he was open to it. The Irishman (A for biggest, most muscled) in the Pen was also (C), the most innocent among us.

"How about 'Shotgun'?" Farmer persisted. "'Buy yourself a shotgun!'" he sang. "Isn't that radical?" he asked.

"Are you saying that Jr. Walker and the All Stars were inciting?" asked Ron. "Right there in full view, in Detroit?"

Or did Farmer, too, know about Sears's basement level and Ron's purchasing a gun?

Ron came to us but never we to him. Maybe trust can only go so far.

NOW, 2000+: The Envelope

I am shocked enough to closely peruse the document. That which startled a day cannot simply be discarded. It vibrates in the room, in the memory.

The envelope is a C minus, picked at, the sticky parts not sticking, the clash of colors and inaccurate rules. The flap is merely glued shut, no metal clips to secure it.

The paper is a D—xeroxed from an original (and where is that?). It's white, not yellowing from those decades ago. The Xerox picks up creases and tears in the original, pages bent in corners. It has no special smell—Xerox doesn't, unlike the rag content of books that intoxicates us into reading. The typeface is something like Times New Roman, printed in bold, fourteen point. There are the dark shadows of the copying, the casual strokes of lives reproduced, and then the black, thick as Magic Marker, of obliteration.

An odorless, anonymous, intimate package on my doorstep.

I open the door and look down the street. Who brought it? The postal person? Delivery person? Still raining and only car traffic, no pedestrians outside.

I become terribly worried. Has someone got more on me? Will there be further packages? We have all dispersed, I and my colleagues, to where tenure was offered, notoriety was forgiven, or where we went underground. I wonder, did our Bullpenner who went underground know of this relentless tracking of one's life?

But the disappeared will appear after we've almost forgotten they had gone away.

I bolt the door and draw the drapes so that the already dark room cannot be traversed without light. I turn on the master switch. There are pools of light under the lamps. The package casts its own shadow. I open it nervously. I am greeted by "Criminal Investigation Division" heading the first document in boldface, as well as the date: **August 10, 1965.** Something bold was being revealed about the past and repeated in the present.

THEN, THE SIXTIES: The Times

Nostalgic, not only the politics but the noisiness of it, the groups, communes, communities. Herds and hordes coming down the road, hitchhiking, farming in New York, pioneering in barren states. And the clothing. Tie-dyed, long skirts, miniskirts, farmer shirts, macramé vests, leather, and jeans, the jeans dressed up with silk blouses, the jeans dressed down; clothing modest and long as an Amish woman's garment, clothing with peekaboo holes for breasts and navel. Abbey Road, and London clothes of jackets and caps from old uniforms; the wide lapels and ties and the flared pants. That was a time of flare and hair.

Hair—face hair, curly, curly hair, long hair, unshaved legs, the Afro, like a warrior's helmet, or straight hair floating in the air as the young danced. Generous hair in the armpits and pubic hair braided, loose, long skirts twirled. And music. Every action to music.

I was, as never before or after, so in the swing of things: unruly hair, dancing to the Oud in Greektown, drinking ouzo. It was the time of ethnic: American Indian, Greek, Black, and Appalachian.

Hope. Never forget hope. "I can't live if I can't hope," said our poet in the Bullpen.

And, then, hopelessness.

And it was "all across the nation . . . people in motion," going to San Francisco with flowers in their hair (Scott McKenzie).

There would be my students dancing at a Greektown festival, flowers in their hair, candles in each hand. And then absent from class.

Their parents would call me. They had taken off, without a cent.

"In the early morning rain," Gordon Lightfoot wrote, "with a dollar in my hand . . . with no place to go."

Another parent phoned, always the mother, with the father on an extension.

"She didn't say a word before she left," said the mother.

From his distant extension the father would grunt, "Not a solitary word."

"Are you going away with no word of farewell?" wrote Tom Paxton in "The Last Thing on My Mind," ". . . Not a trace left behind."

I began to cry to music.

Those years turned out to be for us, the new instructors in the Bullpen, hip and happy but also sad and surprisingly dangerous.

T̶H̶EN: The Underground Railroad

I reread Dostoyevsky's *Notes from the Underground*, after the disappearance of our friend (about which more in due time), to comprehend the locale of "underground."

Not "dugout," as in *O Pioneers!*—which we taught in American lit—Willa Cather's immigrant farmers sheltering themselves in a pit dug into the hard ground of Nebraska.

Nor basement apartments, which more than one of us had to rent in the sixties, located on a bus line to the university, our window a display case for shoes, sandals, thongs, gym shoes, Cuban-heeled shoes, black wing-tipped men's, oxfords, galoshes.

"Underground" could be memory of the storage room in our parents' cellar, the walls lined with canned jars of pickled cucumbers, plums, applesauce, cherry jam, or peeled tomatoes that glowed when the cord to the dim lightbulb was pulled.

Underground, in the sixties, was also the Underground Railroad, the means of secret transport of draft dodgers (to you), conscientious objectors (to us), through the tunnel under the Detroit River or over the Ambassador Bridge to Windsor, Ontario, in southern Canada, or through Buffalo to Niagara on the Canadian side. If it was autumn, we would tell customs that we were on an outing to see the migration of the monarch butterfly from Point Pelee, the southernmost tip of the country.

After leaving off our charge, we would make our way through a dense fog of butterflies smashing against our windshield or under our tires as we skidded over them. And still they flew through the air like autumn leaves, gathering for the flight to Mexico.

The fugitive(s) we delivered would, we hoped, connect up with supporters and stay clear of both the hurtling butterflies and the Canadian Mounties.

The Bullpenners were not unanimous in this action. One of us had an orange VW Bug. The car's owner was ungenerous in the loan of it and kept the information of meetings with fugitives secret from the Bullpen. Did he distrust one of us, and why did he come to trust me?

(Later, when I had already walked the plank of instructorship and was an assistant professor at Slippery State Community College, I used a different Underground Railroad, the Jane Route. For five years, I put my young students on a bus or a train, bound for Chicago to those self-taught providers of safe abortions. Along this route, campus ministries supplied the addresses, their ministers and rabbis frequently apprehended for breaking the law. But why do I "paren" these remarks? This is a matter of history, of which the Red Squad was well aware.)

As for our friend, our missing friend, out of our own Bullpen, he was located in that amorphous, changing, desperate place of the underground.

THEN: Partying

What do instructors, graduate students, and adjuncts do when they're not correcting papers, preparing lectures on their specialty, if lucky, or working on a new approach to a course, assigned over and over? They're studying for orals, researching their dissertations, and going to the optometrist for thicker lenses. But more. They're partying.

Our big parties were at the home of the Farmers, a woodframe two-story which abutted the freeway. It was an old Detroit house, memento mori of a once-good neighborhood. The house trembled with traffic or wind.

"Do you know the history here?" native-born Kevin asked me. He tells. "The city was torn asunder by General Motors, The Chrysler, as we called the factory, as well as our city's royalty, the Fords. Why did they wreak havoc?"

"Why?" we all asked.

"To bisect the neighborhoods so the city would be a highway to the suburbs. Where they lived."

His old mixed Polish-Irish neighborhood was destroyed. The grocery store on one side of the superhighway, the residents on the other; the church in one place, the congregants across the highway, unable to reach it.

"Destroying communities," Kevin said, "to fill the coffers of the automakers is sinful."

I had never heard him political and bitter before.

O'Dwyer was listening. "I have a solution. Flood the expressways," he said, "and turn Detroit into Venice."

The Farmers were generous to their envious Bullpenners who hungered for home and family. In high school we had committed ourselves to ZPG, Zero Population Growth. If we kept true to our pledge, did that mean the rest of us would have no marriage, no offspring, and, maybe, never a home?

THEN: More Partying on Down
1. A Halloween Party

First Prize: The Expressway, a sandwich board, worn by the amateur harpsichordist, on which a map of the expressway was mounted, with glued-on toy cars, some realistically stalled at expressway entrances. Perhaps our friend was looking for a fast getaway.

Second Prize: *The Scarlet Letter*, Mrs. Farmer as the repressed Reverend Dimsdale and Farmer in drag as Hester, the adulteress, an *A* hanging from a chain around his neck.

Third Prize: *The White Sheik*, our priest-on-leave in whiteface, silent-screen lover in an early Fellini film. Did our Kevin have time for the temporal before he committed himself to the church, or was his love of the sacred? Did he know about love aside from the sacred? Or had he been too young when he committed himself?

Fourth Prize: Sancho Panza and Don Quixote ("quix-ot" as the English department arrogantly insisted upon calling him). Ron was with us then, the knight, short but grand with helmet, sword, and shield (courtesy of our theater department), jousting with the imaginary foe. Our pale poet, O'Dwyer, was his Sancho, subservient, foolish. I didn't know he could act so convincingly.

The prizes, from first to fourth, were heavy metal address plates that hung around the necks of the winners and clanged as they cavorted.

2. A Ph.D. Party

Jack Bernstein took off to New York for two days to defend his dissertation ("The Contemporary Writer as Exile"). Upon his return, he described to the Bullpen what had happened. He was dismissed from the room after his defense while the committee decided on the merits of his work. Bernstein waited in the hall outside of the conference room. The door opened; his dissertation adviser extended his hand: "Dr. Bernstein, would you join us?"

We applauded.

So, of course, we of the Bullpen gave a major party. I, Anka the Greek, found a humongous real trial balloon, which we air-pumped the whole day so it would be fully inflated for the party. The plan was to fasten the balloon, as ostentatious announcement of the PhDeification, to the front porch of the Farmers' little house off the downtown expressway. The great balloon would bang against trees, upper-story windows, and bob high above the roof and oncoming traffic. As a final touch we decided to print CONGRATULATIONS, BERNSTEIN, in giant strokes with black Magic Marker. When the chemicals of the marker touched the rubber, the balloon slowly deflated. Bernstein watched in horror, the wrinkling, curling rubber crowding in upon itself, encircling, fizzing, jerking, a startled jump, and then lying there in a pool at his feet, like a giant used condom.

This was not a good omen for Bernstein.

"Bernstein," the Bullpen had asked, "what do you want to do with your phid?"

"Be a shepherd on a kibbutz," he said.

"But why the phid?"

"So they'll call me Dr. Shepherd."

(That was not quite a topical reference to Dr. Shepherd of Cleveland wrongfully accused, in the fifties, of murdering his wife.)

Ah, Bernstein! A deflated balloon, a sick joke. What will happen to you? None of us quite anticipated Dr. Bernstein's future.

3. Black Bars

Ron came in for long weekends to make it to the parties.

"Missed us," Farmer teased. "To leave civilization for the outback."

Ron did miss Detroit, "where music was the main thing happening on the scene."

He would show up with old 45s of songs that Smokey Robinson wrote for Mary Wells, "The One Who Really Loves You" and "Two Lovers." Ron and O'Dwyer would turn chairs upside down and drum to the Miracles; Little Stevie Wonder, the blind boy; and Martha and her Vandellas.

"Look what I have," said Ron. "Just released, the Four Tops with 'Baby I Need Your Loving.'"

We at the university were only a mile downtown from West Grand Boulevard, where this music studio was taking over the street, one building at a time. Everything surrounds us, and we are unaware of the very air.

When Ron came in we went to Baker's Keyboard Lounge, a mile from Palmer Park, where my basement apartment was located. I was at Woodward Avenue, the main drag, and Seven Mile Road, a mile from Eight, where the city ends. Even that close, I'd never been to Baker's before.

With Ron Ivory we would hear the Funk Brothers, backup for Motown: drums, keyboard, and guitar.

"Who's the white guy?" Ron asked the barman.

"He's tight with them," said the barman. "Moe, on keyboard."

"Does the rest of the country know about this music?" I'd ask.

"Beginning to, Anka," said Ron. "But soon they'll rename the city for it."

I am near but far from the action. The park along Woodward Avenue separates me. My neighborhood, I was told by Kevin, was once pastoral. There had been pony rides for children. On tree trunks were little cards identifying their Latin names and native habitats. But the blight came, said Kevin, the Dutch elm disease. Where there had been shade there now were stumps. As the city left for the wealthier suburbs with healthier trees, the park suffered.

Even so, when I paused from grading papers or preparing lectures in warm weather, I would hear the quacking of ducks and the honking of horns and geese. Through my window wafted spicy smoke from the barbecue pits. When I left the apartment house, I would see children lining up at the refreshment stand, old men resting on folding chairs when they weren't playing bocce.

In winter there was an ice-skating rink over the pond. As the city thinned, I began to think of the citizens ice-skating their way out of Detroit.

Although the police station was about half a mile down Seven Mile Road, the park at night frightened me. The refreshment stand was boarded, bocce players homebound, the trees sparse, and the snow dirty. I feared driving home from late classes and, even more, parking in the dark lot behind my building.

At least once during the night a squad car would wind its way around the park. The cops never left their car. Small animals scurried from the sound of the motor. The precinct declared the park safe. I was unconvinced.

But when Ron came, it was the liveliest city anywhere.

"Come more often," I told Ron. "I miss you."

"'Reach out and I'll be there,'" sang Ron. "'Ooo-oh yeah, I'll be there.'"

But he wasn't there. Not often enough for any of us.

"'Baby, don't leave me,'" sang Farmer, either sincere or mocking; one never knew. "'Oh, please, don't leave me, all by myself.' The Supremes."

"You're not by yourself, boy," said Ron. "You've got a missus and a half."

Ron never took to Farmer. Nor did Farmer ever take his missus anywhere.

On the weekends of those visits, O'Dwyer's face would be flushed, his stance jazzy. But by Sunday night and Ron's return to Brahmin Land, O'Dwyer would become a humped-over, pale male.

Ron came in as long as O'Dwyer was with us. Both were gone from view by the time the sound of Motown was the only sound around.

THE SIXTIES: Laughter

I, Anka Pappas (ABD: "The Influence of Ancient Greek Drama on the Modern Playwright"), had a new student to amuse the Bullpen. He was Mr. Berger in my creative writing class, who served as my continuing character for the whole semester.

"Tell a Mr. Berger story," said Joe Farmer (current dissertation topic: "The Countryside in Modern American Literature").

We loved nothing better than stories. Our parents had long

since stopped reading to us at bedtime. Our students were our major source of tales.

There was no space in the Pen to gather. Celotex boards divided us, with our own stories, emblems, anthems pinned to the boards. Kevin's division was unornamented, not religious, political, or sexual. Not past or present. In limbo, though I believe the church has done away with such a state.

Three of us had idealized young women, Farmer with airbrushed Varga girl pinups. "They're classics," he grandly informed us. Two others had calendars of girls engaged in agricultural pursuits. Bernstein's was of a red-cheeked young woman, wearing kerchief and overalls, reaching high to pick the apples from a kibbutz orchard. My muses of the Greek calendar had glossy curls and rosy cheeks, dimpling as they picked grapes from the vineyard.

I also had a black-and-white postcard from the British Museum, of the "Elgin" marbles kidnapped from the Acropolis by Lord and Lady Elgin. "Get Them Back!" was my mission and motto.

I feel that way about a lot of things.

O'Dwyer's single photo was of the poet Garcia Lorca, pinned at eye level in his cubicle. Ron would often roll his swivel chair to O'Dwyer's cubicle.

"Mr. Berger!" my Pen mates reminded me.

Stuck in place, they inclined their heads attentively.

"Assignment," I began, "a descriptive scene. Mr. Berger entitles his scene 'The Loss of Innocense,' of course, misspelling 'innocence' along the way."

"Pretty good. That means he's read Edith Wharton," said Kevin, our priest in the strict path of leaving the priesthood ("The Sacred in Flannery O'Connor"), but still ready to believe the good in people.

"How would you know about the loss of innocence?" the Farmer unkindly asked the priest.

"Mr. Berger would not know about Edith Wharton simply because Mr. Berger does not read," I said.

"Go on," urged O'Dwyer, a slight blond fellow, quite a good poet, more classical than modern.

O'Dwyer and Ron were two smallish people, pale and ebony. O'Dwyer wrote a series of poems about their friendship, *Chess Men*. The Bullpen funded the first edition by a local press. Between us it quickly sold out. That was before Ron was hired away and the drama began.

"Tell the Mr. Berger," urged Bernstein.

I returned to the assignment. "For the descriptive scene, one kid listed the contents of his bureau drawer. Another one studied her attic. Finally—"

"Mr. Berger!" screamed my mates.

"Mr. Berger said, 'I could not go to the attic or to the basement because only our colored maid goes there.'"

"He said 'colored'?" asked Kevin.

"Unashamedly," I said.

"Mr. Berger continued, 'I wrote a description of something else, but you wouldn't let me read it. You played favorites.'

"Actually, I thought I was saving his ass. Before class I read his piece to myself. The opening line stumped me. Berger began, 'It was a warm, genital evening.'"

"That's original," said Dr. Bernstein, not Columbia—as he would have preferred—but City College. "Give him that."

"So I thought," I said. "But the next line read 'Genital breezes blew.'"

"He can't spell!" said Kevin.

"He cannot," I said, "and did I let him display that ignorance?"

"Nice of you," said Kevin.

I personally had a yen for Kevin but he was sworn to abstinence until his official release from the priesthood.

"So Mr. Berger is sexually obsessed," said the Farmer.

Bernstein chalks up another great remark garnered from our students' compositions and worthy of the Bullpen Award Board: "Genital breezes blew."

NOW AND THEN: The Artifact

I, Dr. Pappas, respected author, lingering on before succumbing to professor emerita, with short full Greek hair becomingly streaked with gray, continue to study the envelope, the container of my activist past.

There are curious line drawings on the lower left of the envelope, a variety of citizens, from children to the bearded, from hairy to bald, gathered before the Congressional Building. An army officer or police sergeant, drawn in darker ink and given more dimensionality in the foreground than the lightly sketched citizenry, is single-handedly guarding the building.

Is this an idealization of what happened in the sixties, that we were free to protest, protected by the strict if approachable officer?

Why doesn't this jibe with my sudden memories: crowd detention in the D.C. stadium, pepper spray in the buses that brought us, the District police with their trigger finger on the spray cans. The ingredients made us vomit on the long trip back to Michigan and clung to our clothing afterward.

"Betrayal" and "traitorous," noun and adjective, were words with which we became familiar as we and our students were arrested on false charges. I will try to do justice to this material, as I once insisted on my students doing if they wanted to get credit for the course. I don't know if credits accrue for memories.

Each day I read the document. There is always something new to be learned. Where was I on a certain date? Whose license plates are listed outside of my house at a gathering? Or, even more triv- ial, a document of my being ticketed for taking a left turn on Livernois "AFTER 5 PM. PROH LEFT TURN." (Would I have been absolved of wrongdoing if I had taken a right turn?) "OPER LIC B-65-6 B 656-745-000-184 EXP 3-10-66."

"BLK HAIR BRN HAIR, 5'2", last address Seven Mile Road, 12/11/65"

Aha! Caught you in a typo. Black hair/brown hair. They meant brown eyes.

Is all the information forfeited then?

I discover more errors. Oh-ho. The Criminal Investigation Division is careless. The very person they are investigating they have misnamed.

In '65 my first sheet from the Police Criminal Investigation Division and Criminal Intelligence Bureau indicated "No record." Then why record me? It also listed my name incorrectly, not as Anka but as "Anchor" Pappas.

My stapled file indicated, on that early date in March, there occurred "unofficial congressional hearings" with the involvement of two congressmen. The file editorialized, "This is . . . an antiwar hearing . . . organized by a group of ULTRA-liberal university professors." "Ultra" capped. ("Ultra"—defined as "immoderately adhering to a belief." Also, isn't Ultra the brand name of a hair mousse, an immoderate mousse?)

The written commentary was followed by a listing of the organizers and objectors, their addresses, past and current.

I read the names down the list. The participants, at first unfocused, then vivid, appear to me, including myself of forty years ago:

I, as PR person, "Anchor," was at the beginning of the list, before the name of the rector, Eugene Gass, of Central Methodist Church, and a couple of assistant professors in history and social studies.

There was one listed as "Very active in the PACIFIST PEACE MOVEMENT, recently lobbied in D.C."

And our Bullpen O'Dwyer was listed menacingly as "a poet

who deals in verse with integration." O'Dwyer came to the gathering out of political conviction, unlike Bernstein, who was there just for me. Even so, Bernstein did not escape denigration: "born in Brooklyn, schooled in Brooklyn, and City College, active in Zionist affairs."

The audience (only 190) was also listed. I sadly remember one name, a member of the public library, social science department: "Subject is the daughter of the late woman [known as] 'the Human Torch,' who set herself on fire in protest against U.S. policy in Vietnam."

Kevin was not allowed to be political. (But he had secret political leanings and, I suspected, he was also beginning to itch for love.)

Farmer, for now, although the most hip of us, was a political conformist and not on anybody's list.

Another, a man, was described as one who "regularly attends SOCIALIST WORKERS PARTY, has been observed in various anti-police demonstrations as well as peace picket lines sponsored by radical groups."

One kindly elderly woman was described thus: "Communist Party related organizations."

There were other police-identified dangerous characters:

Woman who "took part in Anti-American picket line protesting the Cuban blockade in front of city hall, October 24, 1962."

Man, with "brown eyes, bald with fringe of some dark hair, streaked with gray, wears horn-rimmed glasses . . . subject observed in the area but not inside the auditorium."

Student, "is keeping steady company with a colored female."

Man, "both of whose parents were born in Russia; he fought in the Abraham Lincoln Brigade in 1937–1938 . . . expelled from the Communist Party for deviationism.

Has not been seen in attendance in Party circles for
seven years."
Man, "retired from Cadillac Motor Car Company, former
president of Local 22, UAW-CIO."

"Read and Approved by": this was blacked out, as well as the
name of the recipient at the Criminal Intelligence Bureau.

The report mentioned a fascist group, Break Up. The Spy in
our midst quoted indulgently from the spokesman of Break Up
that "the Hearing is filled with dirty, stinking traitors."

I personally recognized the Break Up guy and warned our
chairman of his tactics, to heckle until he disorganized the hearings.

"Watch him," said the Episcopalian priest, Reverend Gass, our
convener.

It was no pleasure to watch the guy from Break Up, with his
pitted skin, thinning hair, and twitching fingers. I alerted the ushers. Break Up, when he wasn't heckling, kept insisting, "Point of
order!" Our distinguished guests, two invited congressmen, did
not sanction disturbance. With much threatening and squirming
and turning around in the grip of the ushers, Mr. Break Up was
escorted out, his boots making a noisy departure. This was my
first but not last experience of his being ejected.

NOV. 2000+: Looking Back

It is interesting to consider who attracted the attention of the Red
Squad.

Our parents may have been born in Russia, or we lived in
Brooklyn and were Zionists or worked at an auto plant and were
union leaders or were white and had an African American lover or
wrote about integrated friendships like O'Dwyer. Or we were

described as balding with a fringe of hair and horn-rimmed spectacles.

I have been standing in my living room, too shocked to sit down. I yield to sudden tiredness. Who put my name on the mailing list, so that, courtesy of Freedom of Information, I am being returned to myself? There is also the matter of added notations by the Spy. Not that the Spy is a quality employee: He/it misspells, uses the possessive pronoun incorrectly ("her's"), and, if a college student, can only be remedial. Remedial but harmful.

THEN: Reality and Fantasy

"A Mr. Berger!" I announced.

We in the Bullpen needed a distraction. Three of us had been summoned to the office of the chairman—O'Dwyer, Bernstein, and myself, those who had attended or planned the antiwar hearings. Herr Doktor's voice soared, and the context of his remarks was clearly heard by his executive secretary and other office personnel. We had overstepped the boundaries separating the ivory tower from the inner city, the disinterested intellectual from the mob. Therefore, we had seriously weakened the possibility of rendering future services to the department.

We three were subdued.

"Serve the Berger," Bernstein said.

Two Mr. Berger Stories

"Assignment: A Mysterious Event," I began. "Some turned theirs in; others didn't. Predictably, Mr. Berger is right on time. Luckily, I skimmed through his mystery assignment.

"'I want to read this time,' insists Mr. Berger. 'You didn't let me read my other story.'

"'We'll have a conference first, Mr. Berger,' I tell him. He sighs heavily all through the class.

"At conference time I have to explain to him that his mystery doesn't work because he has the facts wrong, the physical facts."

The Bullpenners love physical facts.

"'Mr. Berger,' I explain, 'your premise is that the woman character had to be innocent of murder because she could not possibly have had, as you put it, "physical intercourse" with two men on the same day. Therefore, according to you, she could not have committed the adultery of which her husband accused her or the murder of the second man, of which the state accused her.'

"'Mr. Berger,' I say, trying not to be gleeful, 'your character may be guilty of both adultery and murder.'

"'Impossible,' says Mr. Berger stubbornly. 'Why do you treat me this way?'

"'Because you *can* have relations with more than one person on the same day. Take prostitutes—'

"'I refuse to believe this.' Mr. Berger turns his back and pouts.

"'We'll not read this one,' I tell him firmly. 'How about the next?'

"'You promise?'

"'I promise.'"

"You saved him from ridicule," said O'Dwyer. "That was very good of you, Anka."

"I agree," said Kevin.

"But ridicule is the best teacher," said Farmer. "He would never have forgotten that lesson."

"What comes next is worse," I said. "I gave out another assignment: Personify the Inanimate."

"Personify the inanimate," says Kevin, remembering an old

song from when he was up on lyrics. "'Latch on to the affirmative, and don't mess with Mr. In-Between.'"

"I explained, also, about pathetic fallacy, the willows weeping for us, the sky threatening and foreboding. Mr. Berger nodded eagerly. He understands."

My buddies were already laughing in anticipation.

"Mr. Berger does not give me his assignment ahead of time. Instead, his hand is waving in the air.

"'Mr. Berger,' I call upon him as I promised I would."

"That is the danger of keeping one's word," says Farmer.

"Mr. Berger comes to the front of the room. He does not read from his seat as do the others in the seminar. He stands determinedly, his legs slightly spread, the paper clutched before him. He clears his throat showily and begins.

"'Title, "Her Ladyship."' And he continues, 'A hairy, mustached man climbed into Her Ladyship's cockpit.'

"'Excuse me,' says one of his classmates, 'would you read that again?'

"Mr. Berger is not fazed. He reads that opening line again."

My Bullpenners say it together:

"'A hairy, mustached man climbed into Her Ladyship's cockpit.'"

"'But what is animated?' asks another student.

"'The airplane, dummy,' says Berger. 'Her Ladyship, get it?'

"Then the whole class repeats the title and the opening line together.

"'A hairy, mustached man climbed into Her Ladyship's cockpit!'"

"He's ridiculed!" worries O'Dwyer.

"Worse!" I say. "He's invited to join a fraternity. One of the students thinks he's so clever!"

. . .

We stopped laughing. We worried about our students.

Bernstein added this noble line to the other, "Genital breezes blew," on the Award Board.

"'C'mon a my house,'" sang Farmer.

We were incapable of doing anything else. At Farmer's, Elizabeth Farmer, blonde, all-American girl, her face blowsy with pregnancy, half greeted us. She pointed to a six-pack, to the peanut butter, to the white cottony loaf of Wonder Bread, the bakery in this town with the building always surrounded by pigeons and sparrows.

We listened to the Doors, to the bad Beatles bootleg album, to the bad Dylan bootleg album. We were smoking. Farmer tried to persuade the missus to smoke a joint. She refused.

"You're a downer, a real downer, you know?" he said to Elizabeth.

"Besides that, I'm also pregnant," she pointed out, "and we don't know the effects of a joint on a fetus."

"Who's the college teacher here?" asked Farmer.

Mrs. Farmer was also a grad student, distracted from her studies by fecundity. She thought of topics for a dissertation: "The Pregnant Meaning of . . . ," "The Fecund Environment in . . . ," or "Conrad in the Belly of the Beast."

Kevin was sitting next to Elizabeth, neither of them partaking of the six-pack or the joint.

We seldom called our hostess by her given name; to us she was "the Farmer's Wife."

(When Ron was with us he felt sorry for her. "To be subsumed under another's name," he said. "An ordinary Farmer at that." Ron could go on about things nineteenth century. "Another Elizabeth, Gaskell, had to wait a century and a half to get her first name back. All those nineteenth-century women who lost their names, like Margaret Fuller Ossoli, writing under 'Fuller,' listed under 'Ossoli' . . .")

The Farmer mellowed out with the joint. "If someone knocks now, we'll lose our jobs."

"It's so good to be bad," said Bernstein.

"But who's good and who's bad?" asked O'Dwyer.

What we learned was that goodness was no guarantee of good fortune, nor was badness a guarantee of misfortune.

Bernstein was stoned and got into an argument with Farmer.

"Stop fooling around," said Bernstein officiously, "and get your dissertation topic approved."

"First," said Farmer, "it's not your business. Second, Bernstein, how do you expect to stay in academia when I hear there are so many Jews, they're reinstituting the quota."

"Go kiss my mezuzah," said Bernstein.

"Kiss it yourself," said Farmer, "whatever it is."

NOW: Reading about Then; the Files

The entry of 8/1/65:

The "principalls" [sic] are given a file number. Mine is 2164.

That is only one of my many numbers. I am also 1969-M, "Subject's name appears on confidential mailing list of CEWV" (Coalition to End the War in Vietnam), and file number 1123— "Subj. Name appears on list of faculty members from the university active with Coalition to End the War Now."

I can see that I am a confirmed suspect in three separate files of the Police Red Squad, as they call themselves. ("Squad" from Vulgar Latin for "square," and nobody was squarer or more vulgar than they.)

This collection of files comes, not only with duplicates of letters I'd written to the local or campus press and petitions I'd signed but also with notes about overheard remarks: "Subject

refs to the President of the United States of America with disrespect."

THE SLIDING THEN, THE SIXTIES

Wherever we were in '65, we sang from Dylan's "Subterranean
Homesick Blues": "You don't need a weatherman to know which
way the wind blows."

That same '65, the Byrds, Judy Collins, and everyone, solo or
group, sang "Turn! Turn! Turn!"—Pete Seeger augmenting Eccle-
siastes:

> There is . . . a time to love, a time to hate
> A time for war, a time for peace.

By '70 and '71, Motown knew which way the wind blew.

Edwin Starr with "War (What is it good for?)." And then
rhyming "heartbreak" and "undertaker."

Until '71 Berry Gordy held back from producing Marvin
Gaye's "What's Goin' On?" It wouldn't sell.

It sold:

> Mother, mother
> There's too many of you crying
> Brother, brother, brother
> There's far too many of you dying.

Berry had moved out of Hitsville to Hollywood. And so did
Mr. Marvin Gaye. And family. Thirteen years later, April 1, 1984,
the Reverend Gaye, minister of a small church, shot his son to
death.

"Father, father!" sang his son.

There was more than one war going on.

NOW: Exercising Our Rights

Even in my city today we march against the impending war. We are downtown in this college town, a number of us from the university.

As for our employer, once Slippery State Community College, now Southern Ohio University, it has discarded all that once made it accessible to the townspeople. It went up the rungs of accreditation from community college to university, from associate degree to Ph.D. In revenge, the residents still call it Slippery.

There are parents and children among the modest citizenry. Facing us in the square at city hall are tanks, their cannons aimed at us! My state does manufacture tanks, but to roll them down the assembly line and use them against its citizens?

We have ratcheted up events. We are debating whether or not to go to war, and they've already pulled out the tanks. So we'll go to war. (Our town, for one, needs the business.)

When we march again, the campus police and the town police have a plan. We will not be allowed to march along the main street, but are penned into side streets, one group cut off from the other in the adjoining blocks. None of us knows what is happening to the others as we march in place, an hour or more on the side street.

"Who did you vote for for president?" one of my colleagues is asked by a nervy campus cop.

"It's not your business," says my colleague.

It's not the prof's fault that he has a loud nasal voice, which seems to irritate the campus cop.

"Everything is my business," says Campus.

One of my kids, an editor on the school paper, is photograph-
ing. His camera is grabbed and smashed.

"Nazi!" the boy yells.

"I thought they gassed you people," says our campus cop.

This is the new protest—forty years after the old protest.
But they're still singing:

> Mother, mother
> There's too many of you crying
> Brother, brother, brother
> There's far too many of you dying.

THEN: The Bullpen

We were too silent, too serious.

Suddenly, "Tell a Mr. Berger story," said Bernstein.

"I'm tired of him," I said.

"No! *No!*"

"I'll tell about others in the class," I said.

"Are they funny?"

"One is, one isn't."

"Tell funny."

The Funny Story

"Our local supermarket is owned by a Lebanese family. The
owner, knowing I was an instructor at the city college, always
greeted me respectfully. One day he told me that he was sending
his children to college.

"'Make good Americans of them.'"

"All right!" said the Penners.

"I had a fair number of Lebanese students. One day I get a phone call, a high-pitched voice, the mother of one of my students, who was Lebanese but not of my grocer's family.

" 'You take my daughter. You say you educate her. What you educate her for? You teach her to be whore.' "

"What did you teach her?" Bernstein asked.

"I asked them to write about their families." I sighed. "And she did exactly that."

I sighed again.

"She was so proud of doing her assignment that she called the family together to read her homework aloud. The characters in the story gathered: the superstitious mother, ignorant father, hysterical aunts, and violent brothers. I assumed that she was pummeled and unwilling to show the bruising, for she missed the following class.

"But she phoned. 'Not to worry, my teacher. I learned something from this. Don't use your family in your homework. Use somebody else's.' "

"That's funny?" asks Kevin.

"That's the funny one," I said.

"Don't tell sad," says Farmer.

I didn't tell them the sad until later, after it was too late.

The Sad Story, Untold

What I didn't tell was about my favorite student, Big Black Jerome, who often came to class straight off the job, dragging his gear, lights, extension cords, camera. He freelanced for public TV and the Black press.

This was his descriptive assignment for me: he covered a meeting by a controversial person, the Rabbi Meir Kahane.

Big Jerome wrote:

I am blown away by the audiences. There were rabbis and Mrs. rabbis and their fists are clenched for Kosher Power.

I laughed because I've never seen these kinds of folks at political meetings before. Then I stop laughing when I see that the speaker is calling on people in the audience, but he doesn't recognize any of my people with their hands up. Not that he's so good to our Arab citizenry.

Because I'm on the job, I can't ask any questions. So I don't speak.

The back row is made up of Arab students who rise and shout, "Al Fatah!"

"Be quiet," says the speaker, "*Sha, sha,* when I say be quiet, I mean it."

Big guys on the aisle, the rabbi's bodyguards, I figure, edge toward the standing row of Arab students. They sit down. I turn the lights on the audience, which blinds the kids with JDL buttons, sitting in the front row.

I whisper to one, "What's that stand for, JDL?" At first he won't answer me and won't let me photograph him; it's against his religion. That's cool. But someone says, "Jewish Defense League."

"What are you defending?" I ask.

This one guy who wouldn't answer, now turns. "From *schvartzes* like you," he says.

I train the camera on him, on the glare of

his glasses and the white of the little cap on
his head. I catch that insult on camera.

   I finish and pack up my gear and head for
the student cafeteria. I look for a table with
the other cats. I don't feel safe with anyone
else.

Sometime later I read this account to Bernstein.

"It's anti-Semitic," he declares.

THEN: My Protector

There were only two of us in the Bullpen. It was midsemester, and
we were grading compositions. Someone was at the door. My
cubicle in the corner could not be seen unless the person entered
the room.

   The guy hesitated, called out, "Is my teacher here—Professor
Pappas?"

   I recognized Mr. Berger's voice. Kevin looked up, and I shook
my head. He rose, all that height and weight of him.

   "Do you have an appointment?" Kevin asked.

   "I'm sure she'll see me," said Mr. Berger. "I have something to
say to her."

   "I'm sorry," said Kevin, blocking the door. "We're only seeing by
appointment."

   He closed the door on Mr. Berger.

   My knight! Protected.

   "Mr. Berger, right?" asked Kevin. "You'll do the same for me
one day."

   I would protect him. But from whom? His bishop? The remedial students? From Farmer, who lightly mocks him? From his
own self that feels unhoused? From me, who would house him?

NOW/THEN

Dates, penciled in, day and month, as supplied by the Red Squad:

April 13. Ad to support a rally on the mall, paid for by the faculty. [196–, Xerox unclear]
April 17. March on Washington.

And who signed these appeals and ads? They list, and I recall:

a departmental secretary [now dead]
a professorial couple—sociologist and Russian literature [both now dead]
a liberal Democrat, asst. prof of sociology, scorned by the socialists [killed in an auto accident]
another sociologist, daughter of a department store owner [dead of ovarian cancer]
a young historian [who long ago moved to Sweden, where he owns a radio station]
a couple—famous poet married to set designer [split up]
as well as priests and ministers, defiantly signing their names

(Now: our religious leaders have all but forgotten this data.)

THEN: The Bullpen Goes to the Bar

If we had a break in the afternoon, we would head to one of the bars on the campus corridor.

Kevin would come, pour beer into a glass, and drink a quarter of it. Farmer was there first, the papa, gathering chairs for the rest of us. Bernstein was entrusted with figuring the tab.

"It's tradition," said Farmer. "The secretary of the treasury is always a Jew."

O'Dwyer would arrive late and leave early.

"You're like a wraith, man," said Farmer. "You appear. You disappear."

He was gone.

I drank more in that year than ever before or since.

"Anka," said Kevin, very sober and quiet, "will you come with me this weekend?"

"Sure!" I said.

He wanted it clear. "I need something done and someone to accompany me so I'll look less suspicious."

"Hold up a bank?" I asked, giggling from too much beer.

"Something like that," said Kevin, and turned from me.

"'Reach out and I'll be there,'" I sang. "'I'll be there to comfort you.'"

I wasn't the Four Tops, but I was trying.

"The sin of foolishness," said Kevin, walking stiffly out of the bar.

Farmer had been watching us alertly.

"A priest is having a hissy fit," said Farmer. "What's going on?"

THEN: The Hotheads

Because we were young, the police had trouble telling us from our students. Some of the faculty had signed an appeal. We called for regular meetings to augment our size.

(PARTIAL LIST, read our ad in the newspapers as well as in the Red Squad files, as if there were a crowd with their pens uncovered to affix their signatures.)

It was still early in the game, and our colleagues trying for tenure or those tired and long tenured thought we were young hotheads.

In my record I now see penciled: "a crowd of teachers and hippies, and the teachers look like hippies."

That made the few of us even tighter, and the Bullpen, not unanimous in their politics, were like fellow campers, bunk mates, on the same ward in a hospital or prison. So we cared about one another extravagantly and hurt each other excessively.

"Kevin," I said, one of the other rare times when we were alone in the Pen, "if I acted silly, I apologize."

Kevin's head was bent toward his desk.

"Please tell me what you need," I pleaded, "and I promise to take it seriously."

He looked up.

"Not yet," he said.

Grading papers was not his pleasure. First, he had had no practice in teaching and, next, was worried about hurting the feelings of his students.

"If foolishness is a sin," I said, "not to forgive is another one."

A bright smile on Kevin's face.

"Soon," he promised. "I'll let you know."

Why was I so happy when I didn't even know what was going on?

NOW, 2000+: Euphemism

Long ago, Mr. Berger confused "emphysema" with "euphemism." He wrote, "Emphysema is when you use one word to cover up for another."

I am committed to accurate use of language and to the death of euphemism. I worry about the words of war coated with honey. In

Vietnam we had "daisy cutter" and "Puff the Magic Dragon" to depict the effects of explosions.

This is the second war for me that insults meaning.

In this new war, when a bunker full of soldiers—the enemy, of course—are killed, the words to describe their deaths are "softening up." The media are using "attrited" as a verb for the noun "attrition" when they mean "slaughtered." The word "degraded" has another usage, not lowered in grade or humiliated, but used to cover up the deaths in a unit.

The reporters are "embedded," sharing a king-size bed with the military.

In Cuba, the commander of Guantánamo responds to the suicides of three young men: "This was not an act of desperation but an act of asymmetrical warfare waged against us."

Asymmetrical warfare? As if warfare were a symmetrical shape.

In Iraq, a house was broken into by a four-man "stack" of marines, who used the technique known as clearing by fire—"you stick the weapon around and spray the room," called "prepping the room." Seven Iraqi civilians died, including an elderly man in a wheelchair, as the room was "cleared" and "prepped."

I'm here and I'm there and I'm nowhere at all.

Once again, dear Zeus and Athena, there is no one to trust.

THEN, THE SIXTIES

We were romantics. We had a romance about the ethnic makeup of the city, some of us teaching the first Black literature courses, whether or not we were Black. (Ron, when he was here, did not teach Black Lit. The department did not think a Victorian and Decadent studies scholar could also be/teach Black.)

We ate piroshki in Poletown, *pinakatopia* in Greektown, *leben* and hummus with pita in Lebanese restaurants. One in our department, a folklorist from Cornell, studied the Appalachian and Lebanese cultures in transplant. The Appalachians, sharing the same land and tongue, were, as yet, and for a long time after, unassimilated. The Lebanese assimilated in every way but marriage, food, and friendship.

We listened to radio stations specializing in Appalachian ballads, old and new. A new one came from the auto plants:

> *Jesus works on the assembly line*
> *across from me, overtime.*

Or during sports games:

> *Drop kick me, Jesus, through*
> *the goal posts of life.*

So we privileged people over these four years became bluegrass singers, civil rights activists, belly and polka dancers. Some of us almost lost the particular selves with which we had arrived.

What we missed, though, was not ethnicity but family.

THEN: Dissatisfaction

When did disaffection set in? Did it begin in 1965, the year in which my student and my colleague each went down for the Selma, Alabama, march? The student, a grown woman with children, was murdered. My young colleague was so beaten that he died a year later. That same year, another professor at the university, whom we saw off on a Freedom Ride, returned in a wheelchair and has been within its confines ever since. And we are only from the North.

Was it when, across the street from the campus, on the sidewalk in front of the Main Library, a librarian immolated herself, like the Buddhist monks who set their saffron robes ablaze protesting war in their land? That happened on March 16, 1965, when no one knew about the developing hostilities and the country was spelled "Viet Nam."

I led two lives at once: the normal life and the life of headlines.

I prepared for class, drove to work, taught my classes in the same building as the faculty offices. I reached the classrooms along a windowed corridor, with a view of the neighborhood slum. And I drove home past used-car lots, surrounded by a string of chattering, clattering plastic flags, city drab. You knew the suburbs would win.

So, beside the charred sidewalk caused by the conflagration, the news gave off a smoky smell—the napalmed children, and the land itself, formerly "the rice bowl of the earth," now burned rice.

"I can't separate you from the news," complained Bernstein after one of my tirades.

Anger, burning anger, was the suitable reaction.

However, anger was missing from our daily press. Anger didn't sell newspapers. Sex and sports sold. Kevin informed us that there had been a merging of the morning and afternoon presses, the Gannett and Hearst chains. The news was thinned out. As was the editorial body.

"But there's still the *Bulldog* edition," said Kevin, "if you can find it."

"Bulldog?"

"Put out for the miners and foresters of the Upper Peninsula."

Farmer and O'Dwyer found a newsstand that carried the *Bulldog*. They came in waving a copy. We gathered around the front page. The masthead and then nothing but cleavage above the double fold.

"That's retrograde Hearst," said Kevin. "The spot knockers are busy in this paper."

"Spot knockers?"

"Photo retouchers," Kevin explained. "They airbrush out age spots, wrinkles, and freckles."

"How do you know?" we asked.

"An uncle got me a summer job on the paper as a copyboy." Kevin smiled. "I hung around the art department, watching them darken bald spots and put creases into cleavage. It was an education for a young fella."

"Kevin!" I said, leaning toward him, a little cleavage showing.

"That was before I saw the error of my ways," he said.

So that's why double-A cups were busty, and familiar dignitaries suddenly hirsute.

The news was also carefully airbrushed.

The city edition, including national and international news, didn't last a bus ride. That's what my students knew about the world, until the draft.

It was not just anger I felt. Within my corral, I was itching, "setting my trap," as my blessed mother would have called it, for Kevin. He, though lumberingly big, was agile in avoiding entrapment.

And Bernstein was lunging after me! I don't think I was anti-Semitic, but he did seem alien to me both in his accent, his Brooklyn voice leaving off the r's, and in his intensity. He went from excitation to alarm with no modulation.

"You're a crank, Bernstein," I would accuse him after some sarcastic remark he made.

"You got it wrong, Anka," he told me. "I'm Jewish dour, which is something like sweet and sour."

"You're unnecessarily mean," I insisted.

Nor was I interested in the Zionist information that poured from him.

He attempted to be a foreign correspondent, at least a stringer for an English-language newspaper in Israel. He even sent off articles about Detroit, whose Jews were beginning to leave for the suburbs, to be replaced by the Lebanese.

Bernstein wanted to do good works. He would work on the land, he said. He included me. I would love it there! We would volunteer in the summers to help out at the Jewish Institute for the Blind in Jerusalem. He showed me a flyer with a ruby-lipped little girl on the letterhead. He would help her braid her hair. If she can learn braille, he can learn pigtail.

But then he worried. On the advisory board, he noticed, was Dr. Edward Teller, the scientist who fingered J. Robert Oppenheimer. Thus, for political reasons, Bernstein could not help the blind children of Israel.

He handled, juggling different things at the same time. "It's the Brooklyn way," he told me, like trying to sell the Bullpenners tourist items made in a foundry in Israel: trivets, miniature menorahs, a Judah the Lion bottle opener. Nobody bought. Yet it made us all feel like Ku Klux Klanners.

Maybe it was just that Bernstein bored me.

But, in this campsite, one even loved the predictably boring.

Bernstein invited us to his apartment in a low-rent neighborhood. The faucet dripped, the bed slanted, the paint peeled, and a neighbor screamed. Bernstein seemed to have incorporated all of that into his being. He had bitten fingernails. Athlete's foot had spread from his toes and erupted onto his elbow and palm.

"Jeez! Get foot powder," said Farmer, refusing to shake hands with Bernstein.

Even the Farmers had a place that was luxurious compared with this.

Yet Bernstein, with his tired, loopy brown eyes, his wiry hair like rays of sun around his head, even Bernstein was heading toward heroism.

What was happening? Our shapes were changing. In someone's hand, carefully concealed, lay a blackjack. We walked by. Out it came! It left no mark, yet we had been bruised.

THEN: Two Incidents, Shooting and Shocking

I arrived on the fourth floor of the English department building (offices on four, classrooms and auditoriums on the other floors). Those with 9:00 a.m. classes were already there, gathered in front of the mailboxes. They looked horrified. Some cowboy had shot up the place. Besides bullet holes through the metal drawers, the window across from the faculty elevator was also shattered.

"Was anyone shot?" asked O'Dwyer.

We ran to look into opened office doors.

No one hurt.

But who hurt the glass and the metal boxes?

"Somebody wasn't kidding," said O'Dwyer. "It was gunfire!"

I looked to see whose box was wounded. Not the chair's, but one professor emeritus, one distinguished professor, and, of the Bullpenners, Ron and Kevin. Why select them? Racist? Anti-Catholic?

"It makes no sense," I said.

"Maybe it was someone who hated English," said O'Dwyer.

"Everybody hates English," said Farmer.

"But what language do they like better?" I asked.

Could it have been the Lebanese mother and violent sons?

Someone, other than Ron, had a gun. Or could it have been Ron?

That incident only hastened his departure.

Another happening in this time of art happenings. More peculiar than threatening.

All of the personnel in the English department wore glasses, usually a condition they developed, like me, after they started teaching.

The Bullpen was unlocked, as it usually was in the daytime. We returned to our desks from our various classes to discover that all of our glasses (except for those of us who always wore them) were missing. Prescriptions had nothing to do with it: nearsighted, farsighted, astigmatic, weak, moderate, strong.

A buzz down the corridor of our more esteemed colleagues.

"Did you happen to see my glasses?" they asked one another.

"I have thick glasses," said one. "They wouldn't fit everyone."

"Mine are just tinted glass," said another, "so the sun won't hurt my eyes."

On every desk, empty eyeglass cases.

The chair, hearing the commotion, came out of his office.

"Was there an intruder, an unexpected visitor?" he asked.

At that moment, a big guy dressed in fatigues was coming down the long corridor where the tenured occupied the offices. He wore a gold chain from his belt to his boots and an earring in one ear. But he wasn't wearing glasses.

"Young man!" accused the chairman. "Have you been stealing glasses?"

The guy looked startled.

"No, you old coot!" he said.

We were all stunned, hearing the crude disrespect to our chairman. (We only disrespected him behind his back.)

The faculty elevator arrived, clearly delineated: NO STUDENTS OR VISITORS. The stranger hopped in, and the doors closed. It was express from four to one. He was gone and out.

As yet no one had phoned the campus cops.

"Who was he?" everyone asked. "Someone's student?"

"Who would want to see out of our eyes?" I ask.

"Who would want to prevent us from seeing?" asks Bernstein, who badly needed his glasses.

Two unsolved incidents.

Was it a fraternity prank? Just the sixties? Or targeted hostility?

The school paper has the scoop, fresh from the campus:

AN OPTOMETRIST'S DREAM

The glasses are missing from all the faculty offices in the English department.

"It was a glasses thief," the departmental secretary complained.

We have often had occasion to differ with the English professors, with their political naïveté. Now we know, they were nearsighted when it came to world affairs.

This may be a good thing, an admission of shortsightedness, myopia, or near total blindness when they grade you.

Don't berate yourselves, fellow students. You are twenty-twenty. It is they who are squinting.

The Glasses Thief may have done us a service by revealing what was there but hidden.

Edgar Miller, Editor
Right Thinking

Immediately after this "editorial" appeared, our glasses were returned, none to the correct wearer, of course. But on every desk was the glare of glasses.

We ran up and down the corridors looking for correction, thick lenses for thin, pale blue for clear, astigmatism for nearsightedness. We were jocular, speaking to the senior professors who, before this, had never noticed us.

"Someone wanted to be noticed," proclaimed the senior professor who held the seventeenth-century chair.

THEN AND NOW: The Appeal

THANKSGIVING APPEAL: Mr. President, you have it in your power to give our boys in Vietnam a Merry Christmas. Won't you accept the cease-fire that has been offered?

(Authorized Signatures Follow)

We organized and split the gathering of signatures. I do the Bullpen, defying our chairman, endangering our chances for tenure: O'Dwyer, Bernstein, and me.

I hesitate to accept the signature of a brave high school senior, Jack Tree, who has been teaching young men how to avoid the draft. His principal told him that if he continued his activism, he would be denied graduating with his class. I hesitate, but he insists, and there is his name in the alphabetical listing.

There were neighbors whose names I still recognize, an old-time activist couple who lived in a frame house near my park, the man jailed in World War I for pacifism. Three wars later, the government is still after them!

And the good ministers, lending their signatures as always.

I had placed the ad, gathered the names, and collected the moneys to buy the space. To my surprise, on my desk that day was a five-dollar bill. Only Kevin was in the room.

THEN

There was a knock at the door. (We did have a door!)

Kevin rose to answer.

"Yes?" he asked politely. "Whom are you seeking?"

"Seeking?" said the loud, foolish voice I dreaded hearing in class. "I'm not seeking. I'm looking. For Anka, my teacher."

"And you are?" Kevin asked, looking back at me, hidden from view.

"Mr. Berger," he said.

I am "Anka" and he is "Mr."!

"I'll see if she's available," said Kevin.

I shook my head.

"Sorry. She's tied up," he told Mr. Berger.

"But I'm here already," said Mr. Berger. "I had to walk up four flights of stairs because they told me I couldn't use the faculty elevator."

"I'm sorry, Mr. Berger," said Kevin, sorry he answered the door in the first place.

"Can you deliver a message, then?" asked Berger. "Tell her I don't like the way she treats me in class, and my fraternity agrees with me."

"No, I don't think I'll tell her that," said Kevin, closing the door.

My crush became more serious. All that height and breadth protecting me!

The other Bullpenners drifted into the room.

THEN: Another Berger

"A Mr. Berger Story!" announced Kevin. "But I know only the ending. Anka, tell them the beginning."

"It begins with what I think of as a very civilized gesture," I say. "The class is three hours long, once a week. We get weary. Mr. Berger kindly offers, 'Let me bring the coffee. Let me, please!'

"'Certainly,' I tell Mr. Berger.

"Mr. Berger rises, takes out a pad, a small dime-store sharpener, sharpens his pencil on the table in the seminar room, while we all watch the pencil curls falling. Mr. Berger moistens the tip of his pencil.

"'How many coffees?' he asks. 'How many coffees with sugar? How many coffees with cream? With both? How many want a doughnut? Sugar doughnut? Plain? With chocolate?'"

My Bullpenners are an appreciative audience.

"Twenty minutes of the class passes as he writes down vital information."

"How many in the class?" asks Bernstein.

"Twelve, that's all."

Screams.

"He departs. We wait. He is gone quite a little while so we commence a story. This is a personal recollection of a child going to a kosher butcher shop. We hear the gory details, still clear in the middle-aged student's memory. She is coming closer to the climax of her story when Mr. Berger returns.

"In an emotional voice, she reads, 'So, what was once eating the green grass, is now strung up on a conveyor belt.'"

Inappropriate laughter from my colleagues. I continue.

"Mr. Berger is very quiet. He sees that he is interrupting."

"Mr. Berger is improving," says O'Dwyer.

"The reader is getting to the conclusion. She keeps licking her lips and watching Mr. Berger, who tiptoes, so carefully—

"But Mr. Berger has leather soles that echo. He pulls out a chair. It has an uneven leg. The chair rocks."

"Stop! Stop!" says Kevin, strangling and coughing on his laughter. He pulls out a hankie (not a tissue) and wipes his eyes.

"Mr. Berger," I continue, "then puts his tray of coffees on the table and places a napkin over one arm like a waiter."

Bernstein says, "Better and better."

"There is Mr. Berger with his new fraternity pin, feeling very fraternal. He carefully studies the cups that are unmarked, lifting the lids and spilling, whispering, 'Who had just black? You, I forgot.' He is passing the styrofoam cups down the table, while my poor reader is trying to conclude, 'And so I will never eat meat again! Never ever.'

"While Mr. Berger asks in earnest thought, 'Who was sugar?'"

"Didn't you say anything?" asks Kevin.

"I didn't say. I bellowed. '*Mr. Berger!!!*'

"'Next assignment,' says Mr. Berger, 'you won't give me such a hard time about reading out loud.'"

"That was the ending?" asks Bernstein.

"No," says Kevin. "The ending is, he came looking for her, with the blessing of his fraternity, to complain about mistreatment."

"He could report you," says Farmer.

"For what?"

"He's in creative writing. He could make it up," Farmer tells me.

. . .

It's ten to the hour, time between classes. The others have left. I rise from my desk chair and head toward Kevin, who doesn't have a class that period.

"My hero!" I say.

He stands up, all of him, and bends to kiss my cheek.

"I just don't want to have to protect you all semester from Mr. Berger," he warns.

THEN: Back to Childhood

The holiday season. Christmas, in fact. I'm Greek Orthodox. That is the state church of Greece, although I'm not of that state. Even in my home state I was isolated.

There was an Orthodox church on the outskirts of our town—old-timers and no one near my age. They seemed a little too full of iron, the Iron Cross of the Second World War, and, since then, had allowed no young priests into the monastery.

In my childhood, I was aware of the occasional Greek name—on a leaflet, running for city council, or on a billboard with a smiling Greek announcing a car franchise. The weather woman was Greek, a great triumph! To have one of us predict sun or sleet, even if she showed no signs of her origin: Nice 'n Easy blond hair, thin eyebrows, and a perfectly shaped body for all kinds of weather. The Greek proprietors did not announce their names on signs above their diners, calling them instead Park Side or Riverview, though no park or river was in view.

After my mother's death I seldom went home. If I stayed away she would still be there. When I did return during winter or spring break, I found the neighborhood the same but the neighbors different, as well as the occupants of my own home. My father's two sisters had moved into the building of four-apartment flats, with an extra bedroom to care for their brother. The smell of cooking was familiar, though, olive oil, garlic, eggplant, and lamb.

THEN: Little Mozart

Next door had been a Jewish boy, a year or two older than I, with whom I played Monopoly all summer long. In games we were equally matched, but, otherwise, we were not regarded as equals. Joseph was a piano prodigy who performed and toured, wearing a velvet suit with a jabot. He was billed as "Little Mozart." On special occasions he played at school assemblies. His mother showed me a poster of him, in profile, wearing the fancy outfit.

When I was close to beating him at a game, I would tease, "You're losing, Little Mozart!"

He hated it, the name, the suit, maybe the whole thing.

I'd be sitting in my shorts on our screened-in porch, swinging us both slightly on the glider. Joseph had the same four-family flat setup next door, but we had the glider and the screened-in porch. The glider would glide; my legs would swing. One day, he reached over and touched my thigh, then higher.

"Are you crazy?" I slapped his hand away.

The next day he whispered, "Did you ever play doctor? You have a basement, don't you? We could go down, and I'd show you this whole new game."

I was curious. My father was at work, my mother shopping.

"Okay," I said.

The basement was no fun. A storage room for canned applesauce, jams, pickled vegetables, the wringer for sheets and towels, a dim light not to waste electricity, and a little floor space in between.

He took towels out of the laundry basket.

"They're dirty," I said.

"It doesn't matter," he told me. "Lie down."

"I don't like to lie down. I don't even like to sleep."

"This will make you feel so good," he said.

I lay down on the dirty towel, and Joseph rubbed me between my legs.

"Feel good?" he asked.

"Funny," I said.

"Take off your panties, and it will feel better," he told me.

Since he was a genius and a prodigy, I took off my panties. He began rubbing.

"Good?"

"Better."

Joseph starts to take off his pants. He has them down to his knees when we hear the screen door slam.

"Anka?" calls my mother.

I can't speak. Not at all.

"Anka?" She's anxious.

I can't speak.

"We're here, Mrs. Pappas," said Joseph, his voice a little high. "It's just cooler in the heat."

Mother is quick down the stairs. Joseph is dressed by then, I'm sitting up, and the dirty towel is back in the laundry basket.

"What were you children doing?" my mother asked, her voice cracking.

"Nothing, Mrs. Pappas," said Joseph.

"Go upstairs," said my mother. "And don't ever do it again."

He went home, and our Monopoly was over for the summer.

By winter Joseph became a bully. He would wait for a snowy day, then go inside to get ice from his refrigerator and wrap it in snow. He threw snowballs at me all the way to school. I would be cut and bruised and crying by the time I arrived.

"Who did this?" asked my homeroom teacher.

"Joseph Stein," I sobbed.

"Little Mozart? Why would you make up such a story?"

She would send me to the principal, who called my parents to school.

"It's jealousy, sheer jealousy," said the principal.

"Are you jealous of him, my sweet one?" my mother asked.

"No," I said, "I don't even like him. In fact, I hope he dies."

"See?" said the principal.

At last my mother and angry father went next door to complain.

I heard my mother at Joseph's front door. "I want to complain about two things," she said, and the door closed behind her.

I wasn't hit by snowballs anymore, but he called, "Crybaby itsy sucks her mama's titsy" every time I passed him by.

"Little Mozart, Little Mozart, all he does is play and fart," I said back, but nobody thought it was funny.

I haven't played any games since, not cards, not board games, not even sports. Doctor I didn't play until I was a sophomore in college.

Everything is dangerous. I might get hit by ice concealed in snow.

What happened to Little Mozart? He simply melted away.

Childhood is a small town.

A bad cold was developing. I was leaving earlier than I had intended, my father driving me to the train station. We gathered in the living room for good-byes.

"So, when will we celebrate a wedding?" asked my father.

"Your father says you share an office with other nice intelligent professors," said one of my aunts, the eldest sister.

"Two of them unmarried, he tells me," says the younger sister. "You got a choice."

"Just choose before I'm dead," says my father, picking up my suitcase.

THEN, THE SIXTIES: The City

Here in Detroit, we Greeks spread across the city and suburbs, our professions proliferating—from the academic directory to judges to columnists. However, we have no Greek predicting the weather.

In the inner city itself more stores than Greeks are left in Greektown. We have souvenir shops, our bakery and church. We buy the special pastry and hold a candlelit processional, chanting our way to church. In the popular consciousness, this does not compare with "Silent Night" playing in all the department stores or that lumpy, dumpy "I Have a Little Dreidel" that Bernstein sings on every occasion.

The artifacts of my office are few. On my desk, I have a modestly framed snapshot of my modest mother, her hair pinned in place. She would have disapproved of me, my basement apartment, my late dissertation, my drinking at the campus bar, my longing for a Catholic, my bushy hair and eyebrows, even my unrestrained laugh. I know this, though she has gone the way of the gods.

Next to my desk, sitting on its haunches, is a leather briefcase with gold initials. My father presented it to me with a little bow when I was hired by the university. "Don't carry your lunch in it," he said.

Above my bed, in my basement apartment, is my Greek cross,

different from the Roman, with the post and crossbars the same length. My family, my history.

My identity.

THEN: Protest and Holiday

Going with the Bullpenners for Christmas Eve was like being a real American, even though it was our same old mixed bag that had been invited. The Farmers were very involved in Christmas, besides expecting their baby any moment.

I arrived late, having marched in an antiwar parade at sundown. The parade began where all the city's peace and civil rights marches originated, at the Central Methodist Church, downtown on Woodward Avenue. There was no sight of the sinking sun, however, for the sky was gray and the air heavy with moisture. Nor was there heavenly sympathy for the pacifist cause. It began to rain and then to pour. I did have an umbrella but inadequate boots. When the march ended, an hour later, my umbrella had turned inside out and was like a tulip bulb collecting rain. My boots sloshed water, and I began to cough. I had no time to change from my soaked clothes.

The Farmers' place was like one of those houses/apartments around campus, lived in by every instructor signed on for a four-year contract. Each added nothing nor took anything away. But maybe because of Elizabeth, the place was pleasant. The bookcases were of raw lumber, separated by glass bricks. Milk crates were end tables, lamps were bulbs covered by photographers' aluminum reflectors clipped onto a pole or shelf, flea-market unmatched dishes made for dinnerware, and jelly glasses sufficed for wine. Rag rugs lay on the painted floors. And it was homey.

The Farmers had invited us for wassail. They provided the gallons of apple cider. Kevin prepared the ingredients to heat up at the Farmers'—the spices, the roasted apples, the sugar. O'Dwyer and Bernstein brought the liquor. We arrived in excitement. But Elizabeth was weary and distracted, holding on to her belly. She sat unmoving on a kitchen chair.

We tossed out every pot from the cupboard until we found a large cauldron for the holiday fare.

"Food, Mrs. Farmer!" demanded her husband. "Where's the food?"

She waved him away.

The tree in the living room was unusually decorated. The branches, laden with glass telephone insulators, were heavy under the weight. Farmer removed them from the tree and made a green glass circle around the trunk. He loved those relics that fell from telephone poles near his farm.

"The rural life is the true life," he often proclaimed.

He read the essays of Southern poets—Allen Tate, Robert Penn Warren—about the corruption of cities and the purity of the country. "Cosmopolitan" was the curse word.

"Cosmopolite" for Bernstein had bad historical memory, an adjective that insulted Jews.

"Why is urban so blighted and the countryside so pure?" he asked Farmer.

"That's the way it is," said the country boy.

This Christmas Eve, Farmer had an inspiration and placed candles in the insulators.

"Missus," said Farmer, "we'll light them for you and the baby, and expect it to show up on schedule."

We decorated with more Farmer artifacts: a fox skull he had found near the railroad tracks in Iowa City, where he was studying. And on top, he hung a spelling-bee medal shaped like a star.

ELIZABETH BENTLEY was engraved on it.

Why did Elizabeth Bentley sound familiar?

"I was once a spelling champ," said Elizabeth Farmer. "And I once had a name."

She had such elegant features that her bulging belly seemed as if it belonged to someone else.

We hung strings of popcorn and cranberries from the branches. As further decor at the base of the evergreen, Farmer had confiscated a traffic light, a danger signal, flashing on/off; on/off. We were yellow; we were dark.

We got darker. All the insulators were now cracked from the heat of the candles.

Mrs. Farmer began to moan.

"It's all right," said Farmer. "They're only insulators."

Kevin looked up at Farmer, who was taking a toke.

"Can I do anything?" he asked Elizabeth.

She shook her head.

"'Hello darkness, my old friend,'" Farmer Simon-and-Garfunkeled it.

"I changed my mind. Please help me upstairs," Elizabeth said to Kevin.

Kevin helped her slowly climb the stairs. Her head rested against his chest. He stayed a while and then came back down.

We were wassailing, caroling, generally making noise, when, at a moment between songs, we heard screaming.

"The wife," said Farmer.

"Go to her, man," Kevin ordered.

Farmer did but came down fast.

"It's gross!" he said. "That hairy head stuck right there between her legs."

I rushed up. Elizabeth was grunting and pushing until the head emerged amid blood and placenta.

"Call the hospital!" I cried to the group below.

We wrapped her and the baby. Farmer's old car was in the garage getting repaired. Kevin threw Farmer the keys to his Volkswagen. Only room for the Farmers and the new Farm product.

We sat around aimlessly until Farmer returned.

The baby had been born at home. Because she had pine needles on her from the blanket under the tree with which we wrapped her, the infant was put into the Dirty Baby Ward.

Mrs. Farmer remained in the hospital in Maternity, the baby in its separate section. We toasted the father, the mother, the holy dirty child.

Bernstein said, "I'll take you home, Anka."

"Not necessary," I said, my eye on Kevin.

But Kevin never competed.

Bernstein had a typical instructor's car, like Farmer's, whose motor intermittently started and stopped. He bought it fourth-hand from a line of instructors who were denied tenure.

"She feels rejected," Bernstein explained, not referring to Mrs. Farmer but to his car. "I can't press her too much. Maybe I should stay over in case she can't make it home."

By now I'd developed a deep rumbling chest cough.

"Or maybe not," said Bernstein.

Feeling low, I rearranged my apartment. I slept on the couch in the living room to be close to the phone.

O'Dwyer phoned. "Use Vicks on the chest and a vaporizer," he said.

From Bernstein's instructions, I made a "goggle moggle": hot milk, honey, brandy.

I phoned the Farmers. The phone rang and rang. Elizabeth Farmer answered, "Hold on," and forgot about my being on the line. I'd begun to blur in her memory.

Kevin came over with supplies—tissues, aspirin, various cranberry, orange, and grapefruit juices, and, tucked into the bag, a soft stuffed giraffe. He left the bag hurriedly and departed. I was contagious in every way. Kevin was having a nervous time, regarding the church, separation, and what he called civilization.

"I don't think I'm meant for this," he said. "But what the hell *am* I meant for?"

For me.

I was doubly lonely and isolated in my apartment. The city frightened me. Kevin, a native son, informed me that Detroit had been the bottom of an ocean, eroding into this flat place. I felt landbound though we were landlocked.

In the winter the city was deserted. The park loomed across the street. I would hear the scrape of skates on ice or the occasional shout from a snowball fight. But at night in the Motor City, nobody walked, and the sidewalks were empty. I was officially one mile from the edge of the city at Eight Mile Road. Did the city drop off the map, off the four corners of the earth? I was on an ancient sailing vessel, and around me blew the angry face of the North Wind.

What I did not do was prepare lectures or grade papers. I also did not leave my apartment. I waited indoors for the vacation to be over.

"Mama!" I call. I've called out to her a lot lately.

She doesn't seem to hear me.

"Goddesses!" I plead. They're even older, further removed.

THEN: The Action

The semester began with an action. I had an invitation from Reverend Gass, the clergyman who called himself an activist-pacifist.

We were to drive up to Midland, Michigan, to picket the Dow Chemical Company.

The photographs were being published in the press. When we invaded another land, that was abstract. But when the war invaded my dreams, that was real. This ingenious company had invented a plastic that not only burned but clung and continued to burn. Company headquarters was practically in my backyard.

I crammed into a little car, not Bernstein's, not Kevin's, but the Errand of Mercy car, Reverend Gass's car, the name painted on side doors. The few of us who showed up fit into the car, though our pickets didn't. The sticks were in the trunk with our rolled-up signs.

"Propitious time," said Reverend Gass, "a shareholders' meeting."

Midland city police and company guards were in the parking lot and surrounding the building. We had intended to invade the meeting, rising, exhibiting our signs. One was BURN, BABY, BURN, of a Vietnamese child hideously scarred. We also had blowups of melted hands, of an infant and mother fused together. GUERNICA, the poster read.

"Where's that at?" asked a shareholder.

The police had forbidden our fastening the signs to the pickets, so we stood in the cold, the cardboard flapping.

The shareholders, whom we had hoped to stir and influence, were outraged by our presence.

Every war, I learn, is prep for the next; yet each in turn is forgotten.

The cops closed in on us, spray cans and nightsticks aloft.

"This calls for calm," counseled the reverend. "Practice passive resistance."

Going limp, the whole nation will learn, only serves to further irritate the police. We were dragged and dumped into the paddy wagon, booked but not jailed.

"Nevertheless, we have made a statement," said our optimistic minister.

NOW/THEN

I realize now that, although no one heard a statement from us, our protest was leaked to the right-wing campus paper.

The next day in the campus press the Bullpenners read of the attack on the "Pitiful Four" who picketed:

> . . . leaving the scene of the crime, and making a farce of everything they're connected to. That some of them represent the university is unfortunate.
>
> Edgar Miller
Editor
Right Thinking

Some of them? One of them. Only I.

That irritating article from the student press, the "Pitiful Four," is in my files, with bold typeface: **"Detroit Police Department Criminal Intelligence Bureau, October 25, 1966."**

Of course I wrote back to that pompous shit:

> Dear Editor Edgar Miller,
> *Right Thinking*
>
> I suggest that in the future the campus press consciously employ staff members who express all points of view of the student body.

I further suggest that we, as a university, refuse to allow any manufacturer of germicidal or chemical warfare products to appear on our campus to solicit our student body in their immoral pursuits.

Yours,

Anka Pappas

(Hello, here it is in my files: "Detroit Police Department Criminal Intelligence Bureau, October 31, 1966.")

A few days later, the office was empty except for Kevin and me. I was finishing grading before class when again there was a knock at the door. Kevin waved me down as I attempted to rise without displacing the papers on my lap.

"Yes?" he said. "Down Chemical? As in 'Down syndrome'? You want the medical school."

He closed the door, then grinned at me.

THEN, AGAIN

The aura in the Bullpen was suffused with sexuality. Bernstein was homesick and, therefore, lovesick. Farmer's wife was recovering from childbirth, and he was getting horny. Kevin was becoming twitchy and had taken up smoking. He fixedly stared at the Celotex board of his cubicle as if it were a window to the outside world. This, instead of working on "The Sacred in Eudora Welty." He seemed to me less sacred than secular, but he was fighting it all the way. Nothing operatic or dramatic was happening. As yet.

Kevin dressed formally, long-sleeved white shirts and ties, substituting one costume for another. When the cubicle was air-conditioned he wore his sleeves down and buttoned at the wrist. When we were airless, the sleeves were rolled up. He was muscular from his sports life before seminary. His arms were smooth with light hairs. His hands were long fingered and graceful. Even his elbows were sexy.

Katherine, the French princess in Shakespeare's *Henry V,* learns a few words in English to speak to her suitor, the parts of the face, the fingers, and the "bilbow." She touches her elbow. I so admire Kevin's bilbow!

O'Dwyer dozed at his desk, startled awake. He rose and lightly touched the back of my neck. His friend Ron wrote and phoned, but his visits had slacked off.

Ron wrote a group letter to the Penners:

They expect too much of me, seeing as I'm the only person of color in the faculty. I'm the expert on everything Black: the campus Black Studies, the Black Students' Dormitory, the Black Poetry Festival. I have a project for a Black Music Festival but no funds to bring in the musicians! Figures!

I hardly have time for my classes. How does one speed read, or expect the students to, through those thousand-page novels of Dickens, Elizabeth Gaskell, Mary Ann Evans, George Gissing?

I'm split—white scholar, Black soul. Like my own name. Sorry to be so down, one and all.

Ron Ivory

"Sorry is not enough," said O'Dwyer.
"Why did he sign his name so formally?" I asked.
"To distance himself from us," Kevin answered.

"Why?" I asked.

"Maybe he knows something we don't know," says the almost ex-priest.

THEN

I, Anka Pappas, since my chances of tenure have become slim, am reckless.

I write another letter to the school paper expressing my irritation at their objection to a DuBois Club Black chapter.

NOW

(There they are with the evidence, true and blue, my guys from the Detroit Police Department, Criminal Intelligence Bureau, Campus Press, date 11/16/66.)

THEN

Dear Editor Edgar Miller,
Right Thinking
(more aptly called *Wrong Thinking*),

If uniformity is conformity, then university is diversity. That means that the John Birch–sponsored American Opinion Bookshop can rent space in a university-owned building.

That also means that the DuBois Club can meet with faculty sponsorship and university approval. Eliminating any one element in the scope of opinions can squeeze all other opinions more tightly together until the difference between them becomes nonexistent.

Anka Pappas

There was a reply, of course, by Mr. Lobschultz, of Break Up, who also identified himself as "the Patriotic Proprietor of the American Opinion Bookshop."

His letter began: "Anka the Greek is a carnival geek."

"Anka, dear," said my bodyguard, "no more letters to the editor. It's over. I've got other things to do with my time."

Most of what he had to do was to meet with the bishop and tell him of his conduct, how obedient he was to his vow of abstinence, how he attended confession, now on the other side of the booth. His confessor frowned upon the fact that Kevin drank a bit, uttered some profanity, and had just begun to smoke.

Cleanliness was almost holiness to him, the twice-a-day shave and shower, the polishing of his shoes, the careful table manners he practiced, and how he cleaned up after himself (so I was told), rinsing socks and briefs in his sink and hanging them over the shower or the radiator. (His domesticity in performing his ablutions thrilled me.)

He had temptations, Kevin confessed, unholy thoughts of fornication, even he confessed, with one person on whom he would like to practice, but he had not succumbed nor did he think, on the other hand, to visit places of seduction. His reading was not titillating or popular, mostly academic or journalistic. He did admit, to his immediate regret, that he was wearying of this long dry spell.

"You chose it!" said his confessor. "You gave up the Lord and His service." A little suffering was good for him.

Some of this he told me. We also shared politics.

"Anka," he said, "there is a group of activist Catholics near the university who support the Catholics in Vietnam and want dialogue with the National Liberation Front."

"Not the U.S. government," I told him. "We never want dialogue."

Our political confiding brought us closer. I listened to his growing awareness, though I would listen to anything he had to say.

"Anka," he said, "I have read reports from New York of priests and nuns pouring blood at missile sites or invading nuclear plants and being arrested."

"That's brave," I said.

"Not for me," said Kevin. "I only recently escaped confinement. I don't want to go back in again." He seemed ashamed. "I'm not brave."

"Oh," I said, "look how you took on the Berger and the Down Syndrome Company!"

"This is no laughing matter," said Kevin. "If you don't take what I say seriously, then don't talk politics with me."

But a minute later, "Do you know that the United Auto Workers, under Walter Reuther, is to the right of the nuns?"

I longed for intimacy in his conversation. Like, *Anka, I've been thinking about you. Our desks are too far apart. I want to connect them. Then I want to lie with you on top of them. . . .*

He opened the large bottom drawer of his desk and stealthily pulled out magazines.

"I got these from O'Dwyer. He's way ahead of me. He looks like a timid guy, but he'll surprise you."

There was a stack of publications from antiwar presses, some with which I was familiar: *The Minority of One; The Reporter; Liberation; Guerrilla;* a mimeographed, stapled series of sheets, *Bring the Boys Home Now Newsletter;* and *Viet-Report.*

"O'Dwyer gets *Studies on the Left,*" Kevin said. "He put in a requisition for it to be added to the university library. The requisition slip was returned from the head librarian and sent to our chair, who vetoed the request. Chair didn't even bother calling in O'Dwyer to bawl him out or explain."

He was obedient to the church and disobedient to the direction of the land.

There were all these new groups out there. "Democrat" was not a new group or a good group because our president wanted to "get the gooks," and the panicky vice president took his orders from the prez. I, from the land that begat democracy, what did I do with my anger, reading this stack of antiwar reports?

"Kevin," I asked this most moral person. "Do we tell the students what's going on?"

He thought about it a long time.

"Yes," he said. "It's our moral duty."

There is a knock on the door. Before we answer the student enters.

"Anka Pappas?" he asks. "I'm Edgar Miller, editor of the paper. I just wanted to know what my opponent looked like."

He looked at me carefully, and then he left.

THEN: Bar Talk

O'Dwyer and I went down Woodward Avenue and into a dive for a drink. We had invited the others. Kevin turned us down. He was having a session with a first-year student. I had witnessed this conferee before, and Kevin was frightened for good reason: the kid was illiterate and in college. But Kevin was speaking to him earnestly, showing him where there was a moment in his paper that worked. Then, in priestly voice, he said, "Poor grammar and bad spelling are not good for you. They're bad for your precious soul."

THEN: The Poet and the Greek

O'Dwyer was pale. His hair was so light that, although he was beginning to lose it, one could hardly tell. He was almost albino. He leaned forward as he walked, eager to get to the next place.

I looked exotic compared with him, his opposite: dark eyed, dark, curly hair. I was passionate, explosive; he pensive and restrained. I knew poets who were explosive, and I knew poets who were restrained. But O'Dwyer was even less than restrained, he was back-of-the-room, last-seat restrained, soft-spoken, polite, heeding rather than heedless, endearing. He was no Dylan Thomas, who had been making the rounds of the campuses in the last decade and whose BBC voice was still imitated by our poets. O'Dwyer could give readings, but one strained to hear him. Unlike Dylan's mining town, unlike Welsh holiday memories, O'Dwyer's landscape was Midwest modest: his childhood—a tire swing, pushing himself aloft on the tire, or round and round, the backyard his circumference. Or the bicycle, his work and leisure implement—the paper route, the neighbors; who paid up and who stalled, the weather, and the condition of the newspaper. And, because he was up so early, reading the paper—all the years of childhood and high school, first thing, reading the newspaper.

> I can't trust the news.
> I can't trust the government.
> I can only trust that my news route
> will pay up,
> that there will be fewer rainy days
> than sunny,
> and my time will be more permanent
> than a headline.

O'Dwyer, speaking quietly, informed me that he was a child of two races. Once he told, his features seemed to alter—his nose widened; his lips were fuller. But it was as if Clorox or Wite-Out had been poured over the rest of him: his colorless, fine straight hair, no delineation of eyebrows.

"It was a clash," he said.

"Does the chair know about your past?"

"He'd never have hired me. He's under the misapprehension that he fired Ron."

Another poem from *Chess Pieces*:

> We're a family with no resemblance.
> I am like my mother with straight
> soft hair
> that disappears when there's light
> behind it.
>
> My brother looks like my father,
> nappy haired, black eyes,
> brown hands.
> We shake hands and startle
> each other.
> How could such mismatch
> be family
> be familiar?

(The next is about Ron. Is this more brother material?)

> He, my friend, was closer than friend,
> more comfortable than blood,
> I knew him from somewhere else,
> a time of childhood we had never spent together.
> His aunts were my aunts

though I never knew their names
and perhaps they would not have welcomed me.
His backyard was a courtyard, a junkyard.
His bicycle was shared with a sister
and then stolen.
That was a tragedy.

Years later he bought a gun.
"I'll know the one who stole my bike,"
he says,
"I'll lie in wait for him.·
I know the one who wants to steal
my mind
my time, the courtyard of my life.
I'll just bide my time,
until he shows up."

Dear Olympians! He knows about the gun! What else does he know?

But then everybody, from Robert Lowell, Anne Sexton, W. D. Snodgrass on down, was writing autobiographical poetry. So why not our Pen mate?

After his recitation, O'Dwyer politely asked me about myself.

"Where do you come from, Anka?"

I don't have the need for confession or the language of intimacy, so I answer flippantly. "I rise from the sea," I told him, "rather, from the seas: Mediterranean, Aegean, and Ionian."

"Quit kidding," said O'Dwyer. "When did you get here?"

"About 500,000 B.C., prehistory. Found with human skull, human activity, evidence of fire. First inhabitants of Europe."

O'Dwyer took a long swallow from his bottle of beer.

I continue, "What we did for the next four hundred thousand years is unclear but about one hundred thousand years ago we had 'shepherds pursuing migrating herds of deer,' as the guidebooks tell you."

"C'mon, Anka—"

"O'Dwyer, do you want to know about me or don't you? We were the first *Homo sapiens*, from which even you descended, and that was about forty or thirty thousand years ago."

"That's good," said O'Dwyer, looking around the bar in case he knew someone else.

I was on a roll. How could he not be amazed?

"There's our art, the wonderful household sculptures of our goddesses, about 3000 B.C., fertility figures you hold in the hand: arms folded across their chests, presenting their breasts, their legs pressed tightly together—"

"I get it," said O'Dwyer.

"And so," I told him, "I expect to be treated with some solemnity, even awe."

"Sorry I asked," says O'Dwyer.

Perversity made me continue. Nobody in the Bullpen had ever asked me.

"O'Dwyer, you asked what I am. What I do. I'll tell you what I don't do. I don't do Greek sorority. I don't do Greek diner—"

"Well, okay," says O'Dwyer.

"You don't know this," I add. "You can't read it in the paper, even the *Bulldog* edition."

O'Dwyer looks confused.

"We don't celebrate your holidays," I said, "because we split from you in the eleventh century and combined with those great nations, the Russians and Romanians. We have been a democracy and then a fascist state and now a democracy again."

O'Dwyer is searching his pockets for a pack of cigarettes. He doesn't find one because he doesn't smoke.

"And why do you think the Right ascended in our recent history? I know this question is on the tip of your tongue. Because we lost so much, so many of our people, half a million, killed in the war, ten percent of us refugees, and thirty thousand children evacuated, many never seen again."

"That's too bad," O'Dwyer mumbles.

"After the war the Right was in control from '49 to '62, about thirteen, fourteen years, until just a minute ago. We hid from them because they demanded that the people sign Certificates of Loyalty, which were not issued for the intellectual, the professional, the activist. I know this from my relatives trying to get out. Without those Certificates of Loyalty we were slaves—couldn't move, work, travel, vote."

"You were a slave?" He has zoned in on a word.

"The people!" I am impatient. "Didn't you learn anything from all those years on the bicycle route?"

O'Dwyer is intimidated enough to wake up. "I never read that in the newspapers."

"Who would print it? The *Bulldog*?"

O'Dwyer ignores my sarcasm. "Why did that happen?"

"Ever hear of puppets?" I asked. "We were puppets of America's Cold War, the southern flank of NATO, and for that we paid dearly. Now, I'm not going to get into Cyprus—"

O'Dwyer agrees, "No, don't go into Cyprus. Let's just drop it, if you don't mind."

"Why, then, do you want to know about me, O'Dwyer?"

"Curiosity," he said coolly, "about a Greek and fellow teacher."

"I'm not a fellow, kiddo," I said. "And furthermore, don't call me Greek. I'm Hellenic, a Hellene."

He's yawning. "Okay, Helen," he says.

My fingers are salty from peanuts, and the table is wet from the beer.

"Back to the stockyards," I said. Rather the Bullpen than dour O'Dwyer.

T̶H̶E̶N̶: O'Dwyer's Story—Maybe

"Wait!" says O'Dwyer. "I didn't tell you about my mother. About how politics were in our lives. How I spent my childhood campaigning for her with my little brother. She ran for Democratic district chairman, for delegate to the Democratic Party Convention. Whatever it was, I was there. I had my bike and attached a wagon with pamphlets. We would go around distributing them, my brother to the Black neighborhoods, I to the white.

"She was secretary of CORE (Congress of Racial Equality) and of the NAACP in whatever town we were living, and we moved around the Midwest while my father had a time, as an educated Negro, finding work that was equal to his intelligence.

"My father said, 'Don't do anything you'd be sorry for.'

"My mother said, 'It's a sorry person who doesn't try everything.'

"My father said, 'Nobody can really see you. They think they can see through you, but they're wrong.'

"My mother said, 'Be open and direct, and people will treat you right.'

"My father went into the clergy finally. His congregation did not accept his white wife and white son. They even looked askance at the Black son. We attended his church, but they were uncomfortable with us and, then, we with them. It was a matter of honor, of pride for my parents to hold this marriage together.

"'Why did you marry, Mother?'

"'Love,' she said, and, 'Hands across the sea.'

"'What?'

"'Connecting two cultures. Showing it could be done.'

"'Why did you marry, Father?' I would ask.

" 'When one is young, one is idealistic,' said my father, 'and thinks nothing of obstacles. Force of personality, of warmth, will work through them.'

"'Did it work?'

" 'Not in most cases. But we persist anyway because that in itself is of value.'

"'Then why did you separate, Father? Mother?'

"'We were tearing each other apart,' said Mother.

"'It was race,' said Father."

We both rest from this family information.

"O'Dwyer, why don't you call yourself by your first name?" I ask him.

"That's coming in too close," says O'Dwyer.

"So who were you closer to?" I ask.

"I was right in the middle, between white and Black," he said.

"And your brother?"

"He knew who he was—in the footsteps of my father."

"And who were you?"

"I was a thespian, playing all the roles. Until I chose my mother."

All of a sudden there are other bodies at our booth. Farmer has come in, strangely dressed for him, in leather vest and cowboy hat.

O'Dwyer looks at Farmer. "New role?"

"It's the papa part," he said.

"And what costume is Elizabeth wearing?" O'Dwyer asked.

"She doesn't wear much," laughed Farmer, "always open-blouse feeding the little critter. Never thought I'd be so bored seeing boobs hanging out there to dry."

I was not too happy with Farmer.

I rose again to return to the Bullpen.

Suddenly, Bernstein and Kevin find us at the bar as I was about to leave. Kevin stopped me.

"But I just got here," he said.

I stayed.

Kevin got the beer, and Bernstein tried to fit into the booth. He couldn't. He took a chair from another table and placed it at the head of the little booth, blocking off the aisle. Customers tripped over him, but Bernstein would not move.

"Did you see the booths in the Student Center?" asked Bernstein.

We had not.

"Tables of anti-Semitism."

Farmer said, "You're too sensitive, Bernstein."

"That's what they told the sensitive residents of the Warsaw Ghetto," said Bernstein.

"They're just antiwar people," Kevin told him.

"You can be antiwar and not anti-Semitic," said Bernstein. "Did you see the cartoons? Shylock making money on the war. Tables from Black Power, Arab Power, all those pamphlets!"

The news was seldom on Bernstein's side.

"Times change." He shook his head. "It wasn't this way during the civil rights movement, arm in arm."

"Shoulder to shoulder and bolder and bolder," sang Farmer. "A Sigmund Romberg operetta."

"Bernstein, a beer?" asked Kevin, who returned from the bar with a trayful of beer bottles.

"I don't really like beer," kvetched Bernstein.

A huge guy coming in tripped over Bernstein's chair.

It was Big Jerome. About to get angry, but then he sees me.

"Hey, teach." He grins. "How come you're hanging out with these down and dowdy dudes?"

"Where you heading, Jerome?" I ask.

Jerome's geniality disappeared.

"An assignment," he said, "my own, and can't tell."

He walked past our booth to a guy at the back of the bar whom he convinced to be a gofer. He waved again as he left.

"Who is he?" Bernstein jealously asked.

"My fave," I said.

"What does your 'fave' call himself?" asked Bernstein.

"Big Black Jerome," I told them all.

"Tell a Big Black Jerome story," said Farmer.

For some reason I had brought my briefcase with me.

"He's too good for you guys," I said.

"C'mon, teach," Farmer mimicked Jerome.

"Assignment," I said, "Innocence or Guilt. Here is Big Jerome's paper. He had been assigned by educational television to cover a trial."

The bar is noisy. Can my colleagues hear me? I want very much to honor Jerome.

Big Jerome's Second Story

We had to leave our gear outside of the courtroom and cover the people who were coming and going, in and out of the courtroom. The short-haired guys with suits were the prosecutors. Long haired, sporty, was defense.

At first I thought it was two worlds, always two worlds, but that day it was still the white world, the White Panthers, white defense attorneys, white prosecutor. Oh, look, up there, in his black robes, the Black judge.

Now that's something new.

All these white dudes are on trial—one kid barely out of high school, picked up for draft counseling other high school kids. He's a smart-assed guy, working at draft counseling since he was fifteen, before anyone else ever thought about the need for it.

But this is a report of what I saw and heard. There is a guy that the trial is all about, Ralph Sincere, and I don't know if that's his real name. He's been in prison, also, for leading the White Panthers. His baby daughter Sunny is there with her Shirley Temple curls passing Life Savers to her daddy. There are these red and yellow candy sugar circles being passed down the long line of fed men with their Primo Carnera faces. (Note to Teach: Carnera, the Walking Mountain, was a world heavyweight champion boxer. You know everything and probably knew this, but just in case you didn't.)

Then there is this high-pitched voice of a blond prosecutor, saying, "Defense wishes to indoctrinate, intimidate, and propagandize. The Life Savers are a ploy."

Ralph Sincere is shaking hands with everyone around the table, his lawyers, his supporters.

The government walks tippy-toe back to the right side of the room. All of the prosecutors are Christian, it looks like. And all of the defense lawyers are Jewish, New York Jewish with long hair and voices they're used to throwing around. One of those Yankees is asking for voir dire, presenting the motion that the defense should conduct the examination of prospective jurors. The prosecutors object that "the defense is asking for preferential treatment."

The judge takes the motion under advisement. Then something big happens. The judge rules on a previous motion. He will not admit wiretapped evidence in the trial!

Defense embraces one another. That is the end of the trial. While prosecution rushes out to phone Attorney General John Mitchell.

Now what is this trial about, I ask you, Miss Teacher? It's about being a federal case because Ralph Sincere supposedly, on the government's word, did one hundred dollars' worth of damage to a federal office, maybe to a typewriter. They can't seem to specify. What exactly had he done? This is besides his being set up on a marijuana rap. One reefer, it's claimed. Lying is going on, my teacher, in a federal court.

I can't use the cameras in the courtroom, but I can afterward. Sunny Sincere has her little arms around her Daddy Ralph and is kissing him with those sticky Life Saver lips. But Ralph is brought back to prison, where he is serving a long sentence on the marijuana rap, and we don't know for sure how the marijuana got there. The feds pull Sunny's arms away from her father, and she screams as they drag him off.

I got it right on film. Innocence and Guilt.

"I liked Mr. Berger better," says Farmer.

I put the paper away and snap my briefcase shut.

NOW

I ponder the words of federal judge Damon Keith: "Democracies die behind closed doors."

THEN: Rejection

The table is wet. The floor is wet. Bernstein is perspiring from sitting in everyone's way. Only Kevin, still standing, touches two fingers to his head in jaunty farewell and leaves. I walk out right after but don't want to call him. I have a little pride. Either he notices me or he doesn't.

He doesn't.

My chest caves in. I cross my arms to conceal myself. Hurt obliterates.

NOW AND THEN

I am reading file 2164.

"Instructor A. Pappas," reads the head, "Wins Award for Story."

Family background acts as the setting for autobiographical story by English department instructor, selected for *Prize Stories: The O. Henry Awards*.

This acclaimed yearly series of collected stories has selected Miss Pappas's story for inclusion.

The narrator is the educated daughter of refugees from ongoing civil strife in Greece. She forges ahead despite the will of her father, walking "against the wind," as she puts it. The narrator is opinionated, rebellious, assertive, as is the story itself.

In the end the daughter wins the grudging admiration of her father, as she earns a scholarship for college. At graduation, the father agrees to stand next to her for a photograph.

The battle seems to have ended but then the father speaks.

"Now," says the father, "it's time to make something of yourself. Get married and start a family."

All that struggle and strife for naught.

Jane Rivers, Student Reporter

Right Thinking

(Detroit Police Department Criminal Intelligence Bureau: April 12, 1967; File 2164)

It is nice to reread the review in my files, but then I am startled, feeling over my shoulder the breath of the Spy, who had written in the margin in pencil "Always the rebel." As if the Spy knew me personally. And then, nastily underlined, the words "opinionated, rebellious, assertive" from the review.

THEN

My chair sent me an interoffice memo in an open envelope that was used and reused to carry messages from one department to another. I was the fifth person down the list.

He wrote: "I read the review in the press. Congratulations on your publication of fiction. Of course, scholarship is the preferable publication."

THEN: Jail

The Bullpenners await the return of O'Dwyer from the White Panther House, where he is giving individual poetry criticism to one of his students. We are off to our favorite dive, and he is later than late.

"He's never coming," I say.

"Give him another minute," says Kevin. "He asked us to wait for him."

"We can meet him there," says Farmer.

There is a knock at the door of the Bullpen. It's Big Jerome. With difficulty, amid the crowding, he makes his way to my desk.

"Professor Pappas," he says (Jerome always gives us a promotion), "something's happened to Professor O'Dwyer. He's been arrested!" He adds, to clarify his role, "ETV is covering it."

Farmer says, "Let's phone police headquarters downtown." He does.

Many calls later, "He's there," Farmer says. "Let's go."

This is during the days of *Class War Comics*, *Libby of Women's Lib*, *Pig Pen* (a commentary on the police), *Kamikaze Komics*. O'Dwyer was also a reader of and contributor to *Kamikaze* along with the student he was visiting. They did editorial work over at the place they called the White House, where, he said, there was always a stack of mags or mimeo sheets, *Fuck You*, *Agnew* or *Ghetto Voice*, talking about the "Brutes in Blue." These data are important because these are the very magazines on display at the police station. I doubted whether the cops had read them. It was enough to display the titles—*Fuck You*, *Agnew*—to show how antigovernment they were, or *Ghetto Voice*, to tell where these dangerous people came from.

Who is showing off? A vice-squad guy wearing blue jeans, a beard, and dark shades covering his eyes. This is the guy who busted both O'Dwyer and the student editor of *Kamikaze*.

Jerome comes along with us, barely squeezing into one of the cars. He describes the earlier scene, as it was reported to him:

"Sirens first to attract attention," says Big J. "Then into the paddy wagon went the Kamikaze Kid and O'Dwyer. On the other end of the ride, my coworker discovered, there had been a lot of phoning ahead, in plenty of time for the AP, UP, and the stringers for national news networks to be there."

The police headquarters is located right in Greektown. You would have thought that the officers, given the opportunity, would have become connoisseurs of Greek cuisine. But they were unimaginative cops who only ordered burgers and fries, even if not on the menu. They did like and bought the knickknacks from the souvenir shops—hard, dark blue sailor hats, Acropolis banks, or Aphrodite ashtrays.

Now the Bullpenners stood in the station awaiting news of O'Dwyer.

Farmer boldly spoke first. "Where's Professor O'Dwyer?"

The Desk said, "No professors here."

I was carrying my leather briefcase with my nameplate in gold letters on the flap.

"We are colleagues of the detainee," I said, professorial pompous. "We demand to know his whereabouts."

"Oh, do you now?" asked the Desk.

"Has he been arraigned yet?" asked Jerome.

"Who is that dude?" Desk pointed at Jerome.

"He works for the university's educational television station," I said.

"I always skip it," comments Desk.

At the moment we heard the snorts and guffaws of the Fink, the guy who had turned in our poet friend.

"You shoulda seen the place, ladies," he said to the officers in the women's division. "Porno is the least of it. The writing on the wall makes our cells look like the Statler Hotel."

The women were shocked. Jerome turned into the room with his notebook.

"Pardon me. I want to get this down right. What place you talkin' about now?" Jerome asked.

The Fink was quiet at the size and blackness of my student.

"The White House off campus," he said reluctantly, not looking directly at Jerome.

"Officer, you're not thinking of the White Tower hamburger joint on Cass Avenue?"

"Not White Tower, dumbo, White *House*."

"The one also on Cass, off campus?"

"Near enough to be a bad influence," said the cop.

"Oh," said Jerome, his face so pure you could bring it to church. "When I covered the place for ETV it was just a plain place."

"Didn't you see the stuff on the walls?"

"Just walls when I was there," said Jerome.

"What's this nigger saying?" asks Fink, grabbing at Jerome. Jerome flicks his shoulders.

Fink takes off his shades. His left eye is cockeyed. We Bullpenners press into the room as Jerome coolly loosens himself.

"The nigger is saying," says Jerome, "that people go there for poetry readings, the New York School, Black Mountain—"

"Get this darky out of my face," says the cockeyed cop.

"What brought you to the White House, officer?" Farmer asks politely.

"The underground," says the Fink. "Following some leads, and what did I find? Plenty of white powder at the White House."

Nervy Farmer asks, "You didn't leak it around when they were out of the room?"

"That's good!" says Jerome, writing in his little lined notebook.

"Desk!" calls the Fink. "I'm being harassed. I can attest that some of these folk were at that place themselves."

As an elevator stops on this floor, an officer prods the occupants out. Among them, without belt or tie or, he later informs us, wallet, is our O'Dwyer.

"What happened to your belt?" I asked, seeing his pants sagging.

"Afraid I'd hang myself," he said.

"O'Dwyer, would you have?" I asked. I grabbed hold of his arm. A cop loosened my hand. He didn't want me attached to O'Dwyer until he was released.

"Naw," said O'Dwyer. "I'd hang them."

The press hung O'Dwyer out to dry instead.

"University professor found in drug den with students" ran on all the wires, TV, radio.

O'Dwyer was being released.

"We've got to get him a lawyer," said Bernstein. "The university has its own lawyer, and O'Dwyer is a paid member of the university community. Right?"

Wrong. University lawyer, she says. "The university is our *only* client."

"Good," we innocents replied. "O'Dwyer is on the university payroll."

"Not for long," says she. "I have to protect the university's reputation."

The Kraut, our chairman, called security to escort O'Dwyer out of the Bullpen. Our colleague emptied his desk drawers into his briefcase so fast that paperclips and lint were gathered up. He tried to stuff the books from his shelf into his pockets.

I wouldn't let security see me cry, but my eyes filled with tears.

"What will happen to my students' papers?" O'Dwyer asked the two securities, who didn't know, and then he turned to us. We suspected the class papers would be divided among us to grade.

"Listen, friend," said Kevin. "Let us know where you'll be."

"Come to my house," says Farmer. He makes the offer comical and more acceptable. "You'd be the most important person in the place, the babysitter."

For the first time O'Dwyer looks as if he might cry.

"Anything you've forgotten we'll send," said Bernstein. His voice was gruff rather than nasal.

I tried to embrace O'Dwyer as he stood stiffly with his stuffed pockets, holding on to his overloaded briefcase.

"But *where* will I be?" asked O'Dwyer, his hair and face so pale he seemed to disappear before he actually left.

We were first dumbfounded, then we all spoke at once.

"He'll go home," said Kevin.

"No, I don't think so," I said.

"She's right," said Farmer, mocking a corny Robert Frost poem. "'Home in disgrace is no place.'"

"He should sue," suggested Bernstein.

"Whom? Whom should he sue?" asked Kevin.

"Whom," repeated Bernstein.

"The university? The Fink?" asked Farmer.

"He should sue the police," said Bernstein.

"It's like you to first think of lawyers," said Farmer.

"What's that supposed to mean?" asked Bernstein. "You with your super-Trojan-size anti-Semitism!"

But Bernstein forgot his ongoing feud with Farmer. We all had to concentrate on O'Dwyer.

"He has to have his honor back," said Bernstein, "or he will never teach anywhere again."

Kevin seated himself in his swivel chair.

"My God," he said.

He lay his head upon his desk whereupon his phone rang shrilly. Kevin hesitated. With his head still down he lifted the receiver.

"Already?" He sat up. "If you say so. Okay."

"Was it O'Dwyer?" asks Bernstein.

"Phoning from his sleeve?" asked Kevin. "No. It wasn't O'Dwyer."

He swiveled around, caught my eye, and nodded. I rose.

"Where are you two going?" asked Bernstein jealously.

"A secret rendezvous," said Kevin.

I followed him to the faculty parking lot and got in on the passenger side. (I had taken the Woodward Avenue bus to school that day, leaving my car in its unlit spot behind my apartment building.) He backed out, showed his faculty card to the attendant, and then sped us away.

THEN: The Underground Railroad

"We're going to an event at the University of Windsor," said Kevin.

"We are?"

"We and our student," he said.

"O'Dwyer?"

"No, not this time."

"Why do you need me, Kevin?"

"To make it look social."

He screeched his brakes at a series of tenements on Woodward. He tooted. No one.

"Wait," said Kevin, getting out of the car. "He wasn't expecting me to be with anyone."

From the broken door of one of the frame tenements along Cass corridor, a young man came out, wearing a *Cat in the Hat* hat. He had a knapsack on his back. He had kitten-paw gloves, black clothes—sweater, turtleneck, jeans. He looked too solemn to be a performer or party guest.

"Mr. Student," introduced Kevin. "Miss Teacher to you. What name did we decide?"

"Armenian," said the young man.

"How about Katchadourian?" said Kevin.

"Customs may know that name," said the fellow.

"But it will be easy for us to remember," said Kevin.

"And tonight is—?" I asked.

"Literary characters in American literature," said Kevin.

"And we are?"

"Visiting faculty and student from the city."

We did not speak as we drove downtown, high over the Ambassador Bridge into Canada. Canadian customs waved us over to the side.

"Hello, folks," said the customs guard politely. "How long will you be in Canada?"

"Only for the evening," said Kevin.

"You have a social occasion?" the guard asked.

"A co-university-sponsored event," said Kevin.

"At the University of Windsor," I added.

He gestured the young man out of the car.

"Are you also going for the social occasion?" he inquired.

"I'm the entertainment," said the boy. He tipped his *Cat in the Hat* hat.

"Anything in the trunk?" customs wanted to know.

Kevin lifted the trunk. Spare tire.

"Glove compartment?"

Empty.

"What's in your knapsack?" asked customs.

The boy unzipped his knapsack: a regular shirt, a regular jacket.

"My civilian clothes," he said, "for after the performance."

"Anybody have citizenship papers?" the guard checked.

"No. We're American born," we assured him.

"Have a good evening," he said and waved us through.

Canada was always polite.

We drove out of Windsor to a safe place and the boy's next leg on the journey.

"Katchadourian, generally where will you be heading?" Kevin asked the boy.

"The city or the country, as long as it's not the army," he said.

The house did not look as if it were expecting him, but he knocked, and a door opened and closed quickly after him. We drove back, not over the bridge, but through the tunnel under the river.

This time U.S. Customs greeted us.

"Let me see your identification," said Lady Customs.

We both had driver's licenses and faculty cards.

"Why does this gentleman have 'SJ' on his driver's license? I don't see no collar," she said.

"I don't wear a collar," he told her.

"Get out of the car," she ordered.

He unbent slowly, towering over her when he rose.

"What are you doing with a woman?" she asked.

"We're not doing anything," I said, "but crossing the border."

"And that's where it's my business," she said. "I don't want anything dirty coming across the border."

Canada polite. America aggressive. They were building up Toronto while we, "the Arsenal of Democracy," were building an arsenal.

"We have nothing to declare," said Kevin.

"I'm not so sure," she replied.

Without being asked, Kevin opened his trunk, the two car doors, the glove compartment, and invited her to look inside.

This initiative irritated her. She had one thing on her mind and couldn't get off it.

"What are a priest and a young woman doing coming across the border?"

"I'm a priest on leave," he said.

"That's worse," she told him.

She gave us a lecture on morality and how his first duty was to the church.

He glanced at me warningly, not to speak out.

"Yes, ma'am," he said.

She had no reason to delay us further but couldn't seem to wave us on. We stood at an impasse.

"Write down your names and current addresses," she said, "and they better check out."

We filled out the questionnaire while cars began to back up behind us.

"All right," she said. "Move it. But don't tell me I didn't warn you."

The next car closed in upon us. We saw the agent glance inside at the single occupant and welcome him to America.

We were soiled by this encounter and had already forgotten our mission of saving someone from the war machine.

Kevin dropped me off at my apartment. The mile-long park across from my place seemed like the forbidden forest of fairy tales.

"Thanks for coming along," said Kevin, with no gratitude in it, but he watched while I unlocked the front door. Both of his hands were on the steering wheel, and he took off when I got into the lobby.

It had been a C-minus evening, about to become a D.

I opened the door to my apartment. The lights were turned off, all but one forty-watt bulb I used for a night-light. And, dimly lit, under it sat O'Dwyer.

"I called from a phone booth, Anka," he said. "You weren't at home."

"How did you get in?"

"Nothing is hard if you're angry enough," he said.

"You didn't go home?"

"Faculty housing gave me the shove after the university did."

"And your family?"

"Anka?" said O'Dwyer tiredly. "How do you know that wasn't just bar talk?"

I hesitated. After all, he was a poet, not a fiction writer. It didn't seem the time to insist on truth. I could see he was on edge. I didn't want to push him over it by asking how long he'd be staying.

"Should I make up the couch?" I asked.

"No," said O'Dwyer, "I'll sleep with you."

I would rather have had Kevin. Even Bernstein.

"How about food?" I delayed.

"I ate," said O'Dwyer, "hard feta cheese, a can of grape leaves. Mother Hubbard, you have a bare cupboard."

He grabbed my arm hard.

"O'Dwyer, sweet boy, don't do this," I told him.

He put his head on my shoulder and cried. And then he began to yawn.

I pulled him down on the couch and, to my own surprise, softly sang a Theodorakis lullaby. I couldn't carry a tune, but I could rock him, and I did until he fell asleep. I covered him with my chenille bathrobe, then I put on my flannel feet pajamas and climbed into my own bed. It had been too hard a day.

In the middle of the night, O'Dwyer climbed in beside me, wearing my chenille robe.

"No, O'Dwyer."

"It's all right, dear Anka," said O'Dwyer. "I'm not sexually active with women."

In this chilly basement apartment, we cuddled, sleeping in the warm bed all through the night.

O'Dwyer was still asleep when I awoke late, just making it in time for my morning class. I departed school directly after class, stopping at an inner-city market on Woodward Avenue near the university to buy fresh fruit and vegetables, although the supermarkets in the inner city were not so big on "fresh"—you had to go to the suburbs or the Saturday downtown farmers' market for fresh. Woodward went from downtown to the suburbs. I took it to my Palmer Park place.

I parked behind my building and carried the groceries upstairs. The forty-watt bulb was still on, but O'Dwyer was gone.

You would have thought that youth was laughter and chatter. But I attest that there was heartache in the Bullpen.

THEN: The Fourth Estate

The news is reported in the campus press:

> Detroit police are on their guard! English instructor arrested and dismissed.
>
> Instructor encourages student to smoke marijuana in campus hideaway.
>
> Now we have to guard our students against subversive and illegal actions, especially in the English department.
>
> Good Work to you, our guardians.
>
> Yours,
> Edgar Miller, Editor
> *Right Thinking*

THE HISTORIC NOW, 2000+

That night was long ago. My heart still hurts when I remember it. I count other losses as well, through these years, my father and his sisters who were ferried across the River Lethe to join my still-young mother.

How judgmental I was in those days. At my father's funeral I thought of his harsh, difficult manner, of how seldom he embraced me or spoke proudly of me and to me. And yet those remembering him said, "He was a saint. He felt for everyone's pain. He was so proud of his daughter."

I graded C minus for inaccuracy.

And his younger sisters, my aunts, also saints, true-blue and salt of the earth.

Cliché, C plus, I graded.

Now, I wonder, who is left to mark me with a pass or fail?

Those were personal losses, but I also lost icons. The first was the marbles of the Acropolis, stolen by Lord and Lady Elgin. No Greek has forgotten that. We Greeks are suspicious of how the "antiques" were acquired by the Metropolitan Museum of Art in New York or the J. Paul Getty in Los Angeles. One Getty curator explained that these objects just happened to be in a twelfth-century former church she had purchased in Italy. Coast-to-coast looters, we Greeks call them.

We attempt periodically to reclaim the Elgin Marbles. We remind Londoners of how important St. Paul's Cathedral is to them, and how, during the Blitz, every fireman rushed from miles around to pour water onto its blazing roof. St. Paul's remains. London remains.

But our Elgin Marbles are at the British Museum. That's where *they* remain. We are politely reminded of how they would have decayed in the Acropolis. The mighty and kindly British Empire secured and protected them. (Like British Petroleum once protected the oil fields of Iran.)

And here in the US of A, our national loss is the Twin Towers in Manhattan. Even in the Midwest one has images: The blurred shots of desperate people leaping, a tie blown over the shoulder. The bodies making a surprisingly loud thud on the faraway ground. Shoes everywhere. Also, body parts. No intact bodies for the hospitals or morgues.

Of course I phone New York, that is, those I know well and even those with whom I'm slightly acquainted. One story keeps me up at night:

My friend, a lawyer who had changed careers when she was denied tenure at Slippery State, was in a conference room. Her building had windows that looked out at the Towers. People who were forced to jump, the fire at their backs, mouthed *Help me! Help me!* as they fell past the closed windows. My friend fainted. She revived to see her colleagues vomiting, sobbing on the floor, crawling under the long table for protection. But they were unprotected from the horror of helplessness, of pleas going unanswered. It was not their building that was attacked, but an adjacent one. Still, in the panic they had trouble in the long evacuation. Some left and never returned to the firm. Some never again had a night's rest. My friend is traumatized. She either refuses to talk or is doomed to tell the tale over and over.

I am in horror, and, I confess, in terror. But of whom?

A friend, tenured at Colby College in Maine, phoned. Suddenly we're phoning each other, forgetting e-mail.

"The nightmare is everywhere, like when the weather changed after Mount St. Helens erupted."

"You're talking about weather?"

"No. Such a strange thing happened here," she said. "A number of trucks came rumbling down Main Street to our local mall. Signs went up: A NEW YORK FIRE SALE. CLOTHING FROM THE MOST PRESTIGIOUS STORES IN THE WORLD TRADE TOWERS WITH SLIGHT SMOKE DAMAGE. BUY YOUR DREAM BRAND AT WAL-MART PRICES."

"Did you go?" I asked her.

She was ashamed. "I did."

"Did you buy your dream?" I asked nastily.

"No," she said and hung up. After all, she had phoned me to report. She didn't need the nastiness.

I am a freak about detail. I was during the Vietnam time. Data pin down the unacceptable, the unbelievable.

"The firefighters' boots, with four-inch-thick rubber soles, were melting to their feet," shocked *New York* magazine.

Another friend reports from New York:

"The Brooks Brothers store on Church Street became a morgue and way station. I went down with friends to help out with the City Health Unit. Two FBI guys were sobbing and begging us to find their comrade who was missing. The FBI office was in the Trade Center.

"A former fireman came to us, and said, 'My two sons are missing. Both firemen. One has an anchor tattooed on his left arm. I'll just wait here so you'll know where to find me when you locate them.' They were not located and it was a while before the father left."

I read the October 1, 2001, *Nation:* "On Tuesday morning a piece was torn out of our world . . . the heavens were raining human beings."

People are running with their mouths open. People are panting. People are screaming.

From now on we look above at billowing clouds of smoke. War will be the only topic for the next several presidential elections.

But no one will replace the living.

And everyone in the land will be afraid.

And when we begin to lose our fear, our administration will return to the site again and again.

I feel a terrible weariness. I was aroused once before, warned of war once before. I hear martial music again. I hear doubtful information. And I mistrust the same obeisance of Congress.

THEN, 1964

What fooled Congress was the Gulf of Tonkin incident and the "attack" on U.S. carriers. Then came the 1964 resolution to "take all necessary measures to repel attack and prevent further aggression." Every congressman voted for it, and every senator, with the exception of two. And it was fabricated information.

What was real was happening in Motown: Smokey Robinson's "My Guy," written for Mary Wells's twenty-first birthday. "My Guy" was number one pop in May of 1964, the year Johnson was making up resolutions.

Did the president know, did Congress know, that the rhythm in the land had changed?

NOW, 2000+

These days it's weapons of mass destruction. People are booing and blaming the United Nations for lack of toughness, and their weapons inspector, Blix, for not being sharp-eyed and finding the deadly weapons. "Nix Blix," they're chanting.

O'Dwyer was right, all those decades ago, about this: if you're angry enough you can do anything. Like a good Greek, I gird my loins and prepare for Olympic feats.

"We have to march!" I, with my gray-streaked thick hair, say to my colleagues, friends, students.

I tell them, "The world is beyond war. War is obsolete!"

This was all I did by night and day. Phone and leaflet. I had done it before. Why was it so tiring now?

Before, when we went to Washington, the noisy wind would whip the flags. Our amplified voices echoed. But, for ten years, not one of the presidents heard us.

Now we have to be heard. The president is warning the enemy that we will come with full force.

And the enemy sits, looking at the sky, listening to the sea, in every household of old people, their children and their children's children, waiting for the sky to burst open, for the high waves to rise from the sea and drown them.

"Faster!" I urge everyone in this Midwest college town. "There's no time to lose."

And everyone came. On the plaza at city hall the people of the city stood together in strength. Some had radios. "A million are marching in Barcelona. Hundreds of thousands in London, Sidney, Aukland, Alaska, Ankara, and Athens!"

Way to go, Athens!

Eight million chanted, "The whole world wants peace."

There was little television coverage, some of New York, none of the crowd in San Francisco. We didn't even make metro news in our local paper. An international peace movement, and the local media didn't notice.

I address the gathered. "To Washington," I say. "That's where the power lies."

Very quickly we reserve buses, seats on trains, places in cars. Very quickly we leave.

But we weren't quick enough; D.C. is expecting us. They will not allow us to march anywhere near the White House or the Capitol. The police force us down a prescribed street. Ahead of us the cavalry rides its horses. And we, the protesters, are choreographed to march in their shit. All of us—mayors and governors, members of Congress, and we who shuttled in from the Northeast, the Midwest, all have the squishy street, the dreadful odor on our shoes, to bring back home.

THEN: Back in the Pen

The Bullpen had changed. O'Dwyer's desk had not been given to anyone since it was the middle of the semester when he left. His belongings were reduced to a pamphlet on the shelf, seashells, maybe from Lake Michigan, and a hard-brimmed Greek navy hat.

At first we surmised or questioned.

"Do you think he hired a lawyer?" asked Bernstein.

"Unlikely," said Farmer.

We sighed.

"Did he go home?" Kevin asked.

"Not likely," I said. What was home—the story or the denial?

We spend more time at the Farmers', me playing with the holy baby.

"You must be lonely for O'Dwyer," said Elizabeth. "One sweet man."

"Where is he?" I cry. "Where could he be?"

"Call Ron Ivory," Elizabeth advised.

"Who has Ron's number?"

None of us did. Only O'Dwyer had.

In the morning, from the Bullpen, we phoned Ron's university. The operator was not permitted to give out the private listings of the faculty. We asked to be transferred to the English department.

"Who was close to Ron?" asked Farmer.

"I wasn't so close, but I can talk to him," said Bernstein.

Ron did not have classes that day.

"Could you do me a very big favor?" asked Bernstein. "I am Professor Bernstein, his former colleague, and it's important that I reach him."

Farmer and Kevin were gesturing and trying to advise Bernstein, who had to turn his back on us.

"It's wise of you not to give out unlisted numbers," said Bernstein, "and guard your faculty's privacy."

Farmer put a finger into his mouth in mock vomit.

"I have a way to both contact and safeguard him," said Bernstein to the department secretary. "Tell him Dr. Bernstein called and here's my extension at the university. Thank you so much for your help."

"You were licking her," said Farmer.

"Shut up," said Kevin wearily.

We waited. Not long. Bernstein's line rang.

"Ron!" said Bernstein. "How are you, old man?"

(Bernstein's suddenly British?)

"Great! Nothing much to report in the Bullpen. Elizabeth, Farmer's wife, had a little girl. Kevin is still trying to be a civilian. I'm biding my time till I get to the Holy Land. Anka here published an award-winning story. . . . I'll tell her you said so."

We all wanted to talk to Ron.

Bernstein said, "Ron, I don't want to worry you, but did you hear what happened to O'Dwyer? It's a long story."

We sat down impatiently. Bernstein, who was usually such a fast talker, droned on.

"So, in summation, I don't think his life is ruined, just a little gangrenous."

I grabbed the phone and wrestled with Bernstein.

"Ron," I said, "it's Anka. To you too, dear. Listen, we're worried here. Did O'Dwyer contact you? What do you mean, you can't tell me? Is he there with you now?" I looked up at the others. "He says he can't and won't tell me."

Kevin took the phone from Bernstein's desk.

"This is Father Kevin," he said half seriously. "Confess all."

Kevin put down the receiver. "Ron hung up."

"O'Dwyer doesn't want to be found," said Farmer.

"Or he doesn't want *us* to find him," said Bernstein.

"Kevin," I asked, "what is Ron saying?"

"'There's more than one underground,'" said Kevin.

"What's that supposed to mean?"

"The underground of the runaway. And the underground of the pursuer," says Kevin.

"Do you know anything we don't know?"

"Just read your Victor Hugo," says Kevin sadly.

THEN: Funny

Even with our Pen emptying out, we still have a few laughs.

Bernstein is grading papers and shaking his head.

"What's wrong with this person?" he asks. "The one who signs every paper 'JMJ.' I don't have a student listed with those initials."

Farmer and Kevin look up astonished. Farmer laughs. Kevin laughs an octave lower. I don't know what's going on.

"It's from a parochial school graduate," says Kevin. "JMJ, the Holy Three."

"Go to Israel, Bernstein," says Farmer.

THEN: Naming

The Bullpenners are beginning to get on one another's nerves.

Farmer was taking the seasons—or himself—too seriously.

Beginning of spring he appeared as a flower child, in a girlish blouse with a round collar over his jeans.

"Elizabeth's maternity blouse," he identified.

"Haven't seen Madonna Elizabeth lately," said Kevin.

"Nor have I," said Elizabeth's husband. "She suckles the baby, or it suckles from her. They are attached to one another by suction."

"Is that why you're dressing like a little girl?" asked Bernstein.

"F—— you, Bernstein."

There was a noisy crowd in the corridor. A head popped in.

"This must be his dell. Is the old farmer in?"

"In and out," said Farmer. "Where're we going, kiddies?"

Another time, Farmer brightened the early gray days of spring with his Indian wear: a cotton blanket, with Indian designs, spread over his shoulder like a shawl. "The corn dance," he points to two stick figures. "Lightning" to a jagged line.

He wore his long blond hair tied back with a leather thong.

"How!" said Bernstein, raising his hand, palm out.

"Don't be a racist pig, Bernstein," said Farmer.

"But," said Bernstein, "you're a pig in a blanket."

"Out of here, both of you!" yelled Kevin.

"I'm not going anywhere," said Bernstein.

"I am," said Farmer as he left.

"What's going on?" I asked.

Kevin's phone rang. "Elizabeth, he just went out the door—"

Kevin's voice lowered, alerting us. "I'll get back to you," he said.

Bernstein and I both crowded him.

"It's private," he said.

"Not in the Pen," we told him. "Nothing's private."

"What will you get back to her about?" I asked jealously.

"She wants to baptize the baby. She wants me to do it. I'm not allowed."

"But what part will Farmer play?" asked Bernstein.

"Whatever part he wants," said Kevin. "It's his baby."

"What's the baby's name after all this time?" I wanted to know.

"That's it. She isn't named."

An unnamed baby. A beautiful Catholic woman leaning her head against Father Kevin's chest. He will have to name it and comfort her. That's his duty.

My fingernails grow longer and sharper. My eyes narrow. I pretend I don't care. Kevin arranged for a young priest at Jesu Parish, on the northwest side of the city, to officiate.

"What is the little darlin's name?" asked the priest.

The parents stared.

"Holly," Kevin finally said. "She was born on Christmas Eve."

"You're a bit late gettin' around to baptizing her, aren't you?" the priest asked the Farmers.

Farmer, dressed in a suit jacket and blue jeans, was about to object when Kevin thrust the baby at the Jesu priest.

"Take her, Father, and make her proper for us."

Elizabeth undressed her in the chilly stone church. The baby kicked her legs, thrashed her arms about. The priest lifted her and set her gently into the waters of the baptismal font. Holly took a breath and let out a piercing cry. She maintained that volume during the dressing afterward and the thanking of the Father.

Kevin whispered something to Farmer, who shook his head, so Kevin reached into his own pocket to pay the priest.

"Thank you, Father," Kevin said, barely making himself heard above Holly's complaints. "I'm glad I don't do that anymore."

"And what are you doing with yourself, Kevin?" asked the priest.

"I'm being a student." Kevin was diffident.

"Always the good Jesuit," said the priest, seeing us out.

He was anxious to close the door against the wails and travails that he foresaw would follow this prickly Holly.

NOV. 2000+

I teach dramatic literature in Ohio to my graduate seminar, "Classical Roots in Contemporary Drama."

I look through the window of the classroom door as they settle themselves. I sigh. It's getting harder.

I start talking as I enter. "Do you know of the many plays that came out during the sixties dealing with trials? Why?"

They weren't born. Their parents were hardly born.

"Because it was a time of trial," I say. "Do you know who the Rosenbergs were?" Of course not. "Do you know who J. Robert Oppenheimer was?" No.

"They were all Jews," says one of my sophisticated students.

"Do you know of the trial of the Chicago Seven?" I ask.

"Of the Jewish race also?" asks the same student.

Should I begin *Once upon a time*, and upon which time do I commence?

Instead I say, "The period selects the art."

I realize that makes no sense. I try again.

"When everything was under suspicion, the trial form became the dramatic form."

"How would people know about the trials?" another kid asks.

"Newspapers published accounts of the trials. They were our daily documentaries."

I'm older and crankier. Why can't they accept history? Perhaps I'm not teaching as well or as enthusiastically as when I taught that night class in Detroit.

I try to jazz it up for them. I make the mistake of telling them a little of my own life. I tell of the Bullpen and the young instructors crowded inside it, how one of them, a poet, went off campus to a place where students lived and poets read. Someone was smoking marijuana. The law was that if there was marijuana on any floor, all residents and visitors were complicit. So, my Bullpen mate was taken to jail, charged with using marijuana with a student, fired, left us with his empty desk. Into our own isolated academic world, the police had entered.

There was an unsympathetic response to this tale.

"He was silly to visit the student in off-campus housing," says one of my kids.

"They should have met publicly at Starbucks," comments another.

A time before Starbucks, as strange as that seems. A time before cell phones.

"Right," I say.

"But don't you think the police should have been suspicious? After all, where there's smoke, there's fire?"

"What smoke?" I ask.

"Marijuana," says the Jew-identifier.

Are we allowed to be disinterested and disappointed when we teach them? I can't keep up with their music or their language and am even weary, during conference hours, of hearing about first lays and broken hearts.

What happened to idealism? To zeal?

I want to tell them about Big Jerome, but I dare not in case they yawn.

THEN, THE SIXTIES

A young man knocked on the door of the Bullpen. I answered.

"Miss Pappas," he said, "I got a message from Big Jerome. He may be late to class or even miss it, and he says not to worry."

"Now I *am* worrying," I told his friend, whom I recognized as the gofer from the bar. "Why is he so secretive?"

"He didn't let me go with him," said the fellow. "Just set off by his lonesome carrying all that heavy gear."

We were both standing at the door.

"Close the door!" yelled Farmer. "I'm trying to think."

"That's a first," said Bernstein as I closed the door.

In the corridor, we continued talking. Rather, he talked.

"He was all puffed up. He says he's doing something for the community," said the young man.

"Should I worry?" I asked him.

"Yes, ma'am," he answered. "You should."

"It's my assignment to his class." I regretted it. "Writing about community work."

"I wish you hadn't ast him to do that," said the friend. "He's always trying to make an impression, especially on you."

I stayed in the Pen after the others left for the night. The cleaning crew had finished the bathrooms and corridor and was gone. I was still in my cubby.

My phone rang. "Yes?" I answered.

"Miss Pappas," said the voice of the gofer. "Can you come right away? It's Jerome."

I called Kevin and asked him to meet me at Receiving Hospital.

"I can't look at him," said Jerome's friend.

No one could look at him under the sheet.

"Are you acquainted with this Jerome person?" asked the lab tech who was standing next to a policeman.

"I am," I said.

"He had your name on him with some papers," said the officer on the case. "Who is he to you?"

"Friend," I said.

"And student." Kevin believed in accuracy and hated over- or understatement.

"Can you identify him?" asked the cop.

"Where is his family?" Kevin wanted to know.

"Nobody answers the number his friend gave us," said the cop.

"I can also identify him," said Kevin.

Jerome was lying on his back. His skin looked different. The shiny blackness had dulled.

"What happened to him?" Kevin asked after we left the coroner's office.

"He went into a drug den and got the back of his head blowed off," said his friend.

Murder in the Murder Capital. He went off by himself to get material for my assignment.

Kevin was patting me while Jerome lay there alone.

At the wake we passed through the receiving line of Jerome's family.

"I'm so sorry," I said to each person sitting down in the anteroom.

"Who are you?" asked a woman.

"This is his mother," whispered Jerome's friend.

"His teacher and his friend," I said.

"The one who sent him to where he could be kilt?"

"No," I started to excuse myself.

"Don't argue," said Jerome's friend, trying to push me on down the line.

I kept my place.

"He was a great student," I insisted, "a wonderful person—"

The mother shook her head back and forth, back and forth.

"Too late to say it. Too late to hear it," she said.

"Let's say good-bye," said his friend as we lined up for the viewing.

They had dressed Jerome up—a formal jacket, tie, and, where the poor head was flat, a hat.

"Looking good, Jerome," said his friend.

I found a seat. His friend sat with other young people. I was too stunned to listen to the sermon or to hear the singing of the hymn.

When the coffin was lifted by the pallbearers, his mother followed it out, speaking in tongues, cradling, crooning, lullabying him, in the susurration, the echolalia, that sounds before speech.

"Mother!"

It was not Jerome but his father who put out his hand to slow the mother's rush after the coffin.

I looked for something black for mourning when I returned to the office. I opened Kevin's drawer and found a skinny black tie which I taped on the window of our door. I took something out of my briefcase that the gofer had brought me.

After the others came in and settled, I said, "A Big Black Jerome story."

Big Jerome's Final Story, Found in His Loose-leaf and Brought to Me by the Gofer

I know a bad dude in the hood. He's been around almost as long as me. I know he's handy with money. I know little kids are working as lookouts for him. I decide he should not be in my community anymore.

I go to the Main Library and they show me where they have microfilm of old newspapers. I crank away at the machine but don't see his name. I go through some years, then slow down in the present.

I'll have to go to the police and find out what they have on him, but, since Professor O'Dwyer's arrest, I'm not eager to go there.

I figure I'll come in alone and give him a good scare, humped under my camera, carrying my lights and extension cords. I'll tell him I'm just a gofer for local news, and the networks will be coming along right after I set up.

I'll interview him on camera and get him to apologize to the community. Then I'll let him get out of town, out of the hood and out of my face.

Teach, I'll let you know how it works out and I hope it's good enough for the assignment.

Hint, hint, I'm aiming for the High Grade!

B. B. Jerome

In a story inside the *Free Press* I cut out:

KILLING IN DRUG DEN ON TWELFTH STREET

City University student (name withheld because of being a minor) was, according to his friends, out on an assignment to "catch the bad guys in the community." There is no information on where he went or the identity of his murderer. Only the name of his teacher, Dr. Anka Pappas (ABD), is known, who assigned her students to do something that will better the community.

I folded up the newspaper. "It's Killer City," I said.

I left the Pen with dignity, along the corridor to the ladies' room. There I sat down on the dirty sheet that covered the couch and cried. I dared not touch the couch cover or the pillow. Who knew what crawled in while one of us lay there with cramps?

My chairman did not call me in. The university lawyer did not phone me. Whoever has read the metropolitan section of the newspaper is not unduly surprised that a young Black man was killed in this city.

When I returned to the Pen, Farmer pushed away his squeaky chair from his desk.

"The Big Black Jerome story was a low blow for you, Anka. I'm sorry, dear."

That was a surprise. A real person talking.

As always, after Farmer left, his phone rang and rang.

"Jeez," I said.

"Careful," warned Kevin.

"It's euphemism," I said. "Like 'Zounds' for 'God's wounds.' "

"I know euphemism and I know blasphemy," says Kevin.

The phone on his desk rang right after it stopped ringing for Farmer.

Kevin was whispering.

But maybe it's another underground railroad assignation. He hung up and rose.

I half rise also. "Do you need me?"

"No. Little Holly is scheduled for her shots today, and Farmer took the car."

Jeez! "I can take her," I offered.

"Thank you, Anka. I already told Elizabeth I'd pick her up."

I hoped Holly was her noisy self and Kevin and Elizabeth didn't get to say a word between them.

THEN, END OF THE SIXTIES: To Zion

Bernstein, who was never quiet, was crowing, yelling, climbing on top of his desk.

"Yes?" I asked. "Do you have something to say, Bernstein?"

"I'm going! I'm going!" he shouted. "To *Eretz Yisrael*! To the land of Israel."

"What happened?" I asked.

"An invitation!" He's quieted down to a half yell. "An academic conference at the University of the Negev! Their department will pay my way! It's my topic, 'The Jew as Exile.'"

And that's how Bernstein got to go to the Holy Land.

"Are other exiles going too, Bernstein?"

"Oh yes, from everywhere!"

He saw I was laughing. "Wait till *you* get an invitation to speak at the Acropolis or at Delphi," he said.

He was already dancing himself around the room.

He would be hired at the university right after the conference. A faculty member was on reserve army duty. Bernstein would complete the professor's semester and stay on.

"Where is it exactly, Bernstein?"

"Be'er Sheva. The seven wells. Remember?"

"Sure," I lied.

He was about to launch into a biblical exegesis.

"I'll get an atlas and find you wherever you are," I promised.

Bernstein paused. "Come with me," he pleaded. "You're from Greek ancestry, maybe even Sephardic. You could also be an exile."

I was startled. Bernstein persisted, as always. "There are many advantages. You wouldn't have to see the Kraut, or Farmer or Mr. Berger—"

He sang a Hebrew dance song and twirled again. I caught hold of him and kissed him on the lips.

"Yes?"

"No, Bernstein. I love you, but I don't love you."

Bernstein was the third one, including Ron and O'Dwyer, in the diaspora from the Bullpen. It was the end of the sixties, and that left only three of us. We were thinning out: the Farmer in the Dell, Kevin, and me, Hi-ho the derry-o.

And the Farmer takes a wife and the wife takes a child, Hi-ho the derry-o.

And the Farmer neglects the wife. And the Farmer neglects the child.

> *Hi-ho the derry-o.*
> *A friend takes the wife.*
> *A friend takes the child.*
> *Hi-ho. Oh.*
> *Anka stands alone.*
> *Anka stands alone.*
> *Hi-ho the derry-o*
> *Anka stands alone.*

I take out my compact and look in my mirror. I see someone who will continue to be alone, Arachne, a spinster, Spider-Woman, a spinner of tales. Caught in my own web.

THEN: Berger and the Chair

Kevin worked less at his desk. His chosen topic, "The Sacred in Eudora Welty," was set aside. He responded to abrupt phone calls. His presence in the Bullpen was more sporadic.

Hence, he was not here to save me when Mr. Berger came calling to complain about his midsemester grade.

"Nobody in my frat gets a C," said Mr. Berger, red with anger. "I handed in every assignment, didn't I?"

I nodded.

"I was never tardy in attendance or homework, right?"

Again, a nod.

"Doesn't that count for something?"

"You're right, Mr. Berger. In view of the time you put in, let's make it a C plus."

His eye caught our blackboard with the quote IT WAS A WARM GENITAL EVENING.

"I have proof right here," said Mr. Berger. "You don't like me and you're making fun of me."

He began to hyperventilate.

"I'll report you," he said and slammed the Bullpen door. The glass window vibrated.

The next day, unannounced and without knocking, our chairman arrived to question me.

"Mr. Berger is your student, right? What upset him so—the C? He said he was an object of ridicule here."

"Yes," I confessed.

I pointed to the blackboard and IT WAS A WARM GENITAL EVENING.

The Kraut looked puzzled.

"A description of the evening?" he asked.

"A misspelling," I said.

Then the chair read the next line. A HAIRY, MUSTACHED MAN CLIMBED INTO HER LADYSHIP'S COCKPIT.

"Pornography?"

"Stupidity," I said.

"EMPHYSEMA IS WHEN YOU USE ONE WORD TO COVER UP FOR ANOTHER. Also, the same student?"

What was he going to do? Kick me out of the fraternity?

There was a snuffling sound in the Pen. Kevin had opened the door and, in shock, watched the chair.

"Oh!" says the chair. "Make a copy for me. Ha-haaaa! I collect them, too, but these are winners! Wonderful, wonderful!"

His eyes were tearing. He knocked into Kevin on the way out, unaware.

"Guess who's the new department favorite?" I told my Pen mate.

NOV. 2000+

When something bad happens in the capital, permission is given for misbehavior elsewhere.

The mayor appoints a vice squad, SWAT team, with special powers to go into minority neighborhoods and tempt victims. They have their wallets hanging negligently from a back pocket, or they offer to sell drugs to the ghetto inhabitants. In no time at all, several young African American males are arrested, and one immigrant peddler from Africa is shot in the vestibule of his apartment building. The police union defends its members. The officers are not charged with excessive force or with being remiss in duty. They had made an honest mistake with the peddler. Who could tell that the shiny little object in the young peddler's hand was a front-door key and not a gun?

The Student Black Caucus on campus begins the picketing in front of city hall and police headquarters.

I go to picket in memory of Big Jerome and all the others I have known. It is an interreligious group: Baptist ministers in dark suits, Episcopalian priests, men and women, their white collars contrasting with black robes. Large crosses identify them as serious. A liberal campus rabbi is wearing her yarmulke. A Sikh is wearing his turban.

"Justice! Justice!" we shout.

"You're trespassing," say the city police.

"Justice!" we call.

"You want justice," says a copper, "I'll give you justice. You first, old lady."

Old lady? He cuffs my hands behind my back. The handcuffs are tight and chafe my wrists.

"Professor!" calls out one of my students. "How is this different from forty years ago?"

"That was a prequel," I tell him.

My student and I are separated, as are men from women, separated in the paddy wagon and in the station.

We are fingerprinted and photographed. Out of habit, I smile when the photographer focuses on me.

"That's cute," says the police photographer.

Another group has come in, older women, older than I, that is. They don't bother tinting their hair. Some have osteoporosis. They all wear sensible shoes and they are energetic.

"She's smiling!" says one watching me being photographed. "Atta girl."

"Who are you?" I ask the first woman in the new line.

"Who am I, or who are we?"

"We."

"I am Katy. We are the Gray Brigade. Been marching together since 1950 and the Korean War."

"Took three years for a truce, an unsatisfactory one at that," says the second woman in line. "I'm Lois."

"I'm Myra. That was the first of the unnecessary wars in our lifetime," says the third woman, wearing aerobic clothing.

They do history up and down the line:

"In '66, four hundred thousand U.S. troops in Vietnam. Buddhists setting themselves on fire."

"In '68, the Democratic National Convention in Chicago," says Katy, at the head of the line. "We bused in and got busted."

Lois informs me, "Being arrested isn't so much—except in Seattle—but being beaten beforehand, that's a bit much. And the Chicago cops were bully boys."

"It killed the Democratic Party," says Myra, the exerciser of the group.

"In '70—Kent State killings," said Lois. "We in Ohio marched against the National Guard. The kids in the Guard were jealous of the students not serving in the war. They aimed and fired. The governor never took responsibility."

They are the historians of their time.

"She didn't finish telling you about Kent State," says Myra, "Twenty-eight National Guardsmen, sixty-one bullets, four students dead, nine wounded, including one paralyzed for life. This state never got over it."

"Step down," says Desk to me. I hear the group behind me continue their litany:

"All the covert action against Central America. We hardly sat down during that time."

"Remember Panama? You forgot about that one, didn't you?" Myra asks me.

She's right. I did.

"Remember Granada," asks Myra, "pronounced with a long *a*?"

I also forgot Granada.

"We're marching in place," says Lois. "Same people back in power. And how many years do we have left to protest?"

Myra asks me and answers, "Know how many citizens were under surveillance during the sixties? Three hundred thousand! Everybody you knew and their kids."

We are about to sit down on the benches.

"Let's do aerobics," says Myra. "Officer," she tells Desk, "we'll be doing our aerobics now."

Desk looks up startled. The women reach to the ceiling, to the floor; their arms are straight as they do small circles, one way, the other way, counting to fifty with each change.

Desk is distracted by the whirling arms, the counting.

"Hand to opposite toe," says Myra.

Myra looks down at the filthy floors. "No floor work."

Two African American policewomen come out of their office to watch the exercisers.

"Join us, ladies," say the arrested women.

The policewomen look tempted. Desk glowers. They shake their heads.

We begin jumping. Desk gets jumpy.

"Cut it out, girls," he says.

The Gray Brigade surrounds him.

"Officer," says Myra, the hand-to-toe person, "we earned our wrinkles. Don't patronize us. You don't like to be called a boy, do you?"

Desk shakes his head.

"So, don't call us girls."

Lois says, "Look at the signs on the bathroom doors: MEN and GIRLS. That's demeaning!"

The policewomen peek in to see what the argument is about. They grin.

"Just remember, you—," says Desk to us, not knowing how to address this group before him. "No one goes to the john unattended."

The two policewomen say, "We're here, ladies, if you need to use the facilities."

One stands at the open door handing each woman in line a couple of sheets of toilet paper.

"Thank you, dears," say the women.

"Where's their fucking lawyer?" Desk shouts.

"Officers," asks Katy of the policewomen, "you wouldn't happen to have coffee in this place?"

The policewomen look at one another.

"Sure," they say. "Soon," they promise.

In a little while there's the smell of fresh coffee brewing.

The other police come rushing in.

"Not until these women have theirs," say the women officers. "We bought this can of coffee with our own money, plus the milk, plus the sugar and diet packets."

"Hip, hip, hooray!" we salute our policewomen.

It is getting darker in the station, quickly going from dusk to night. We've been here all the day.

One policeman brings in a line of African Americans, handcuffed together.

The first woman in our group looks silently at these arraigned young men.

"What do you do when you see these poor children come in here like that?" she asks the women officers.

"I pray," says the policewoman.

"I talk to them," says the other. "I say, 'I'm praying mightily for you. Don't let it be for nothing.'"

"You're wonderful," Katy tells them.

We're drinking their coffee and schmoozing.

One of the policewomen comes close to us as we wait tiredly on the benches.

"You women are wonderful," she says. "Getting arrested like that. Thinking of my people."

"You lit my candle," says the other.

We almost regret it when our lawyer arrives, an African American woman from the corporate world, doing this pro bono.

"You white women are lucky," our lawyer says crankily. "You've got the food machines and coffee. The Black protesters are in another station and aren't allowed to use the bathroom facilities or the vending machines."

We are being processed out.

I embrace my women wardens, and the Gray Brigade lines up to hug them.

The male officers call. "How about us?"

Desk asks, "How about *me*?"

"You were all gentlemen and we salute you," says Katy.

A few Gray Brigade stragglers are still schmoozing the women officers on their way out of the jailhouse door.

There is a wind, a flurry. A white pigeon is blown in.

"Get that feathered rat out of here!" shouts Desk.

"It's a sign," say the policewomen and refuse to do his bidding.

I return to my own small house, feeling high.

Who says I stand alone?

And I haven't nearly finished my marching days.

THEN, THE SIXTIES

Farmer came in uncostumed, that is, almost normal.

He walked over to Kevin and stuck out his hand.

"Kevin, I want to thank you. I screwed up and you covered my ass."

Kevin looked confused at both the handshake and the covered ass.

"When Holly had her medical appointment and I forgot." Farmer looked sheepish. "You can forget yourself but not your kid. Right?"

"Right," we both said.

"And, Kevin, know that I'll be here if ever you need me. If you get one of those other emergency calls." Farmer paused and sang from Cole Porter, "'It's friendship, friendship, just a perfect blendship.'"

Kevin broke off eye contact. "I'll remember," he said.

"I got a card from Bernstein," I offered, to cut the tension in the air, though I'm not sure why it's there. "This part is funny."

I showed them a picture of Bernstein standing next to a camel. On the photo Bernstein asks, "Which is the more valuable?"

Kevin laughed. Not Farmer.

"I never trusted Bernstein," said Farmer.

"What's not to trust?" I asked. "All he ever wanted was to go to Israel. This part, though, isn't so funny. He writes, 'I thought I'd end up in Jerusalem of the golden stones or in a kibbutz talking to tree frogs, but here I am at the *tuchus* of the state.'"

"Whiner," said Farmer.

I turned away from him. "I liked you better in your maternity blouse."

What I didn't show them was a letter from Bernstein. "Ankale," he wrote, "two books I always have with me, O'Dwyer's *Chess Men* and your story in *Prize Stories: The O. Henry Awards*. I think of us as stuck in time through the sixties, though surprisingly I may have been at my happiest then."

I don't lose Bernstein in all this time, though he may be the most changed of us. We will know each other forever.

THEN, 1971: Another Trial

We three were given annual extensions of our contract. The department could save on an instructor's salary by giving us extra classes and not hiring anyone else.

I had a destination in the afternoon. I didn't tell Farmer. Kevin was out, probably baby tending. I went alone to the Winter Soldier Investigation of war crimes. This investigation took place not far from the university, at a motel on Grand Boulevard.

How tacky, I thought. Especially when I saw the green turf carpet, the rough wooden tables set up for the panels, and the folding chairs for the audience.

Where was Big Jerome when I needed him and his black-and-white television coverage?

Suddenly the room was not just in black and white. It was Technicolor: orange and scarlet, filled with gaseous fumes. Or that's what I smelled when I heard the veterans speaking.

They spoke in neutral tones. Down their cheeks ran neither blood nor tears. These soldiers mourned, remembered, preserved without brine.

The planners of this event, Vietnam Veterans Against the War, wanted to bring North Vietnamese into the country to corroborate. They wanted to bring the North Vietnamese over the Canadian border, across the Ambassador Bridge with the suspicious-eyed border police or through the tunnel under the Detroit River. The USA, protecting its citizenry, did not allow this foreign invasion.

So, who did testify?

I see it as Jerome would, extreme close-up on:

a twenty-one-year-old New Yorker
a long-haired, brown-haired Pole

a captain named Rusty

a straight-haired blond boy, twenty, who had joined the
    marines at seventeen

a check-shirted boy with very black hair and a very black
    mustache

someone dressed somberly like a religious

a thin-faced, densely bearded boy

a fat-faced boy

a wet-faced boy

a former major, cinnamon skinned, now portly, and work-
    ing for the telephone company

a young light-haired boy with glasses

a POW of the North Vietnamese with short hair and a
    lavender shirt

a mixed-race lady doctor with thick glasses

Are there Black brothers, Miss Teacher? Jerome would have asked.
There were Black brothers. And they all spoke of fires:

heat tabs thrown on top of hooches

heat tabs thrown into the camp garbage to burn looting
    children

women and children running from burning villages

the fire of tank, frag grenades, of thirty-cal weaponry

"Willy Peter" that does not stop but keeps burning
    throughout the body

bodies blown away with C-4

anywhere in North Vietnam a free-fire zone

pilots dumping bombs even though told a POW camp is
    located there

Kevin, so learned in God's words, what would you have said?
Kevin would have said:

Those boys behind that long table caused people, animals, and plants to cease their functioning. In that foul and nauseous land of burning straw huts and sprayed crops, the earth was again void and without form.

What would you have said, Bernstein, in the Holy Land?

It was night and it was not good and no one could divide the dark from the light. The dry land was pitted and malarial; the herbs yielded poisoned seed, and the fruit tree yielded no fruit. The heavens dropped exploding light. The cattle and all creeping things were killed.

Says a veteran, with African-black skin, up there at the podium, "Buffalo, plowing rice fields, were frightened by the whirring roto blades of the choppers and ran with their plows, cutting up the fields."

There were rules for the games, the witnesses told us.

"For every ear cut from a Cong, two free beers."

Or

"Setting a dead boy up against a tree, putting a cigarette in his mouth, a hat on his head, a sharpened stick through his chest."

Or

"Blowing away a group of Nam children who give the soldiers the finger."

"CO B carved into a head after it was decapped."

Or

"An ace of spades dropped on a dead nigger Nam."

They told of their experiences.

The former major from Bell Telephone told of torturing with snakes.

Prisoners in wire cages sprayed with mosquito-attracting formula in this malaria-ridden land.

Said a Black brother, "The Nam civs you patted on the head for a trick, kicked in the ass for a fault, and regarded as invisible the rest of the time."

I, a lover of words, heard such words of destruction as "puff," "spooky," and "Daisy Cutter."

Said another Black brother, "All Nams are 'gooks,' 'slant-eyed nips.' Prisoners are 'turd' and 'scum.'"

They began to speak of torture.

"What we do to men, we do twice to women."

When they got to electrical torture I made my way down the uneven row of folding chairs.

I washed my face at the bathroom sink. I dried it on the rough paper toweling, blotting water or tears.

Bernstein, what would you have said?

This is before the Beginning, when life knew no season, no festival, no seed or harvest.

I returned to the conference and stood in the back. The Winter Soldier event was about to end in a curious ritual. Each panelist rose, the woman doctor, the former POW in lavender shirt, the check-shirted boy with raven hair and mustache. They walked in line down from the platform to a series of metal wastebaskets.

"I committed atrocities," said the woman doctor.

"I am William Calley," said the cinnamon major, "who killed five hundred sixty-seven civilians in the Vietnam town of My Lai in 1968. I, too, committed atrocities."

"I am also Calley," said the mustached boy. "I committed atrocities."

And so said the former POW, the New Yorker, the Pole.

There was the explosive sound of metal hitting metal as the Bronze Stars, the Silver Stars, the Purple Hearts, the soldier's medal, the DFCs hit the bottom of the basket.

In a corner, to my surprise, was Farmer, with his head in his hands.

NOW, 2000+ (2004)

The time has quickened in my college town. Events are progressing and out of my control. I find myself panting with each headline. I lie down; I'm too old for this.

No, stay in trim. I take my broken nails and bumpy feet to the salon. The salon is a working-class female world, the beauticians masked against the chemicals of their industry. They peer at us demurely through uncovered eyes, as if under religious restraint.

I have my nails rounded and calluses trimmed while reading *People* magazine, people not in my life or my geography, whose main concern is the gown for the Academy Awards. As a young girl, I read movie magazines, adoring, cutting out photos to tape over my bed, Gene Kelly, Gregory Peck. Now, postmenopausal, I am retreating to puberty.

The salon's air is humid from the frequent hair washings; the clock, on the hour, plays an old sentimental melody.

It's when I leave for the brisk air that I realize how dangerous *People* magazine is, emulated by the serious press, which hires more gossip columnists while calling home its foreign correspondents.

This self-absorption reminds me that I have to become active again.

I fight in the political campaign, do telemarketing to uncertain states, and speak to the citizens: "If you were to vote as of now, would you choose Bush, Kerry, Nader?"

"I don't know anything about Mr. Kerry," my targeted people often say.

I go on bus trips to ring doorbells and ask the citizenry what issues are important to them. My own state is a swing state, and I find myself in a suburb outside of Cleveland.

"Whatever the president wants, I want," says a crew-cutted interviewee.

I follow my street map from green-lawned house to house. KEEP OFF THE GRASS, say all the signs. I realize that anyone with turf will vote Republican.

THEN, EARLY SEVENTIES

After our contracts were temporarily extended, we are warned that this is an unusual arrangement due to losing faculty and increasing the student body. It is also explained, rather severely, we felt, that, after this temporary extension, we will be adjuncts, paid by the class with no amenities. No sick leave, no paid days off, no support if we wish to deliver a paper at a conference. Okay, but would they take away our Bullpen?

ALONG THE WAY: Bernstein

Perhaps I prefer Bernstein in Israel. His letters are never boring, which, I admit, he often was in the Bullpen.

"Ankale," he writes:

I want to write you about a poet, novelist, and rabbi I met and the singer who put them all together in a ballad.

The first was Abba Kovner, the poet, author of Achoti K'tana, My Little Sister, the great and tragic book-length poem about the Holocaust. I took the long bus ride to his kibbutz up north. First thing, he proudly showed me his workroom, separate from his apartment. The kibbutz, he said, honored him after so many years of his fitting in writing between kitchen and field chores. They made him the night watchman so he could write when the kibbutz slept.

It was time for a visit from his daughter who lived in the
Children's House. That was the sacred hour and I had to leave.

I'll continue but I have to quit. I do prepare for class, you know.

Another letter (1974):

My Anka,
In Jerusalem, I met Aharon Appelfeld, a novelist, who, like Kovner,
writes of the Holocaust. Unlike Kovner, a hero of the Vilna
resistance, Appelfeld was imprisoned in the camps as a young boy. He
escaped and hid out for the length of his childhood.

"I never went near another Jew," he said. "They stood out like
scarecrows. I always traveled alone, even though I was a little boy. I
was afraid of the peasants. They were like beasts—they kicked their
animals, beat their wives, slammed their children around.

"I always had to remember my family before I was taken away
from them so I would not become a peasant."

He has not, as yet, been published in English. He consulted with
me about hiring a translator.

"What do you think of this translation from Hebrew into
English?" he asked.

He read, "A smile cracked across his face like an egg."

"Don't hire him," I said.

You will soon hear much of Appelfeld—but not with an
egg-smeared face.

"Anka," he writes, in 1975,

This is a series letter. If I remember, I was recounting the unusual
people I met—poet, novelist, rabbi, and singer.

The café singer is a tortured man (as are many in the land, who
wonder what miraculous deeds they can perform in this mythic

*place). This special friend of mine is a King David, red hair, curly
red beard, young. When he's not composing songs, he's studying with a
rabbi who had escaped the Holocaust. (If you notice from my
previous letters, nothing escapes the Holocaust.) My young friend
took me for a shiur, a lesson at his rabbi's home. His disciples
surrounded him, those who had followed him from Germany and the
new ones from the land. On the dining table before him books were
piled. I could hardly see the rabbi's face. He spoke in a whispery
voice, but the room was so quiet that we all heard him distinctly. And
he taught, opening one book after another, pointing out a word here
that reminded him of another line elsewhere. We left and my
red-bearded friend said, "Come with me to a nightclub and I will sing
you my latest song."*

*And he borrowed a guitar from one of the performers and sang a
song of the land and the people therein, the poet from the kibbutz, the
prose writer who needed translation, and the great rabbi whose soft
voice echoed in his ears.*

*The redhead, gingy, as they're called here, has gone off to
Germany, himself, to get a rabbinical degree.*

*I admit to you, Anka, that I had a yen for the guy. Unheard of at
home and totally unacceptable here. Why was I so shy when he
embraced me, kissed me, nuzzled against my neck?*

Did you suspect this when you refused to join me?

Why, Bernstein, I said, more and more interesting!

THEN, EARLY SEVENTIES

Kevin was preparing for his night class. But he was distracted,
staring fixedly at the view on the wall. I was at my desk, marking
essays. But I froze in my chair. I still heard the banging of military
decorations into the metal basket.

"I did not commit atrocities," I said out loud.

Kevin looked up slowly.

"Of course not, Anka," he said.

"Maybe I did," I worried, "and don't remember."

I started to cry.

Kevin wheeled my chair over to his cubicle.

I cried harder.

Kevin extended two hands to lift me from the chair, as if inviting me for a dance.

I rose stiffly.

Kevin bent me into his lap.

"There, there," he said. "You've been working too hard."

I was not really comfortable pressed against his jacket pocket that was bumpy with pens and pencils. But I would have remained there forever.

Farmer came in.

"That's a relief," he said. "I thought you were after my wife."

We three prepped for class in silence.

I liked the night students. More than in the average class, these night students were Black, older, working all day. Some were on the line, others in the boiler room. They went home quickly to wash and change, but there was still grease under their nails. They were terribly tired but did their homework and showed up on time for each class, trying not to yawn in the overheated room.

How was I to interest them? They were so earnest and yet ashamed that they had no background in spelling or literature. They looked with despair at the assigned textbook.

"Return these to the campus bookstore," I told them. "You'll get others, more interesting. We have a special field of study in this classroom."

Their drooping eyelids lifted.

"What is that, miss?" one asked.

Another bumped the student's arm. "Professor," he corrected.

"We are going to study ourselves," I said.

"That's funny!" said somebody.

"How we gonna do that?" another guy asked.

"By reading the work of others," I told them.

"Makes no sense," someone muttered.

They were defeated before the term really began.

I sat up straight and smiled my most blinding white-toothed Greek smile.

"Class," I announced, "we're going to have such a good time in here!"

They believed me.

I wanted to share my experiment with the class with the Bullpen, but only two warring Penners were there to hear me.

"Kevin," I said, "I'm making a revolution."

"I know, Anka," said Kevin. "What else is new?"

"In the classroom," I told him. "I don't work from the curriculum. I work from their interests."

He stood up, that tall, drafty person, and came to my cubicle.

"Tell me."

For some weeks I tell him.

Sometimes he stands over my desk listening to my recital. Other times he wheels his desk chair to my cubicle.

Oh, Aphrodite, let him learn about my cubicle!

"We're working on a project," I told the night class at that first meeting. They grimaced at "project" . . .

MORE THEN, EARLY SEVENTIES: City Smarts

". . . called City Smarts."

I asked them, "How are you able to live in the city? How were your parents and grandparents making a living? What were their survival secrets? Interview them. How did they get through the Depression, the riots, love and its disappointments, friendship and revenge?"

They listened with their mouths open.

"Ma'am," asks one, who works in a boiler room at the Ford plant. "What does this have to do with composition?"

"A very good question," I said.

He sat up proudly.

"It all has to do with stories, stories told and not yet told. And with collecting them, shaping them so your relatives will be proud of you. Nobody wants a misspelling in their story, right?"

"Right."

"Nobody wants bad grammar in their story."

"No, they don't," they agreed.

Everybody was excited.

"Can it be a book of photographs of the family?" Boiler Room asked.

"Yes, wonderful!" I answered. "As long as the story is there with the pictures."

"Can it be a tape of their voices?" Boiler Room was very persistent, seeing I'm not the foreman.

"A clever addition," I said, "so long as the tape is transcribed."

"Do we read anything?" a student wanted to know.

"You're the real literature of this class," I said.

A Caucasian with a big beard, in his late twenties, raised his hand.

"I don't have family to photograph or interview. What should I do?"

"Interview strangers or yourself," I said.

"I'll do that then."

When I left the classroom the students were either sitting stunned or turning in their seats and talking to one another.

"Oh, Kevin," I said, "it's going to be such a sweet class!"

Kevin lifted my chin and kissed me.

"Sweet," he said and returned to his area of the Pen.

I had new energy. The war was on. The war would be on. But the night class was also on. I put in a special order to the university bookstore for a Harbrace book of grammar. It can't *all* be fun and games.

THEN, 1971: An Incident

And, that very night, sometime after my night class, there was running in the corridor. Few faculty were here this late.

"Don't take the elevator!" I heard a colleague yell. "The stairs!"

No one thought to check on the Bullpen. We were not the most visible members of the department. I rose and looked up and down the corridor. The halls were empty. I returned to my desk. Then I heard sirens and raced out of the room with my purse but without my leather briefcase.

I saw blasts of fire through the windows of the faculty lounge.

Could this be the same person who was shooting up our mailboxes and stealing our glasses?

I took heed of the previous advice and ran the four flights down the stairway instead of using the elevator.

There *was* a fire, in the old gymnasium, now the ROTC recruitment office.

I hung around. No one told me anything.

"Security," said the campus cop when I asked what was happening.

"Security," said one of the firemen.

The campus press, *Right Thinking,* had a banner headline.

UNIVERSITY ENDANGERED

First the ROTC building is bombed. What comes next? Vigilance is in order!

Report suspicious-looking actions to *Right Thinking* and your editor.

Edgar Miller

NOW, 2000+

There are colored alerts all over the land based upon threats to our security. Even here in Ohio.

"The terrorists could be after the tank plants," the mayor explains.

But despite the color wheel I am distracted by an article in the *Plain Dealer:*

CAUGHT AT LAST! WEATHERMAN IS TURNED IN

Long on the list of the FBI's Most Wanted, Jerry Stewart, alias Noble O'Dwyer, has been found in Northern California, hiding for the past forty-some years. He was responsible for firebombing a gym-ROTC building at a Detroit university during the Vietnam War years.

He is being held without bail while friends from his adopted state plead for his release on bail and cite his record as a good citizen of the past many decades.

Accompanying the article are two photographs. One is O'Dwyer as I knew him, poetic pale. The other is the recent "Jerry," shiny bald, bespectacled—the light also glancing off the glasses.

Whom should I phone? Where is Kevin? So sexy, even as a celibate, that he gave pause to the cranky U.S. Customs agent.

Is Ron Ivory still at the eastern university? (Faculty are migrants, academic Okies.) I don't know where Farmer is. Or Elizabeth, and the crying Holly. I care because they were part of my community.

Or is this relativity—the same decade in two lives but in different time frames?

My former chair, I'm sure, is dead by now, buried with his beloved writings from Algernon Charles Swinburne. But you don't know. The young could die young and the old continue to age.

Bernstein! I'll write to Bernstein. He always return-answers.

THEN: A Call

I drove out of the parking lot to my basement apartment. My phone rang as I put the key into the door. I missed the caller. No, it rang again.

"Hello!" I was out of breath.

"You're all right?" a voice asked quietly.

"Yes. Who is this?"

"Your former sleeping partner. Anka, I have to run now, literally. Don't look for me. For your sake. My dear Grecian princess."

I burst into great sobs. What happened? What the fuck happened?

The phone rang again. I was still crying. Maybe it was O'Dwyer!

Tentatively, "Hello?"

"Anka, it's Kevin. I know you have night classes today. Are you all right?"

"Yes," I said, "I got out all right." Then, "Kevin!" I said urgently.

"Anka, what is it?"

To tell him of O'Dwyer's call! But I knew I couldn't, never would. Unpatriotic that it might be.

"I appreciate your calling."

"Listen, my dear, we're buddies, right?"

Wrong.

THEN AND AFTER

"Buddy-buddy," adjective, indicating great friendship. O'Dwyer had been my buddy, if not my buddy-buddy. "Buddy" is also a noun, an alternative form of "brother." Kevin was not my buddy.

Whatever the relationship, Pen mate, bar mate, platonic bed-mate, I had no way of finding O'Dwyer, my buddy. He left no clue, neither name nor whereabouts.

I can't bear to lose people. I don't have that many to spare. My chest hurt me for at least a year.

As a scholar I tried an archival approach. What poetry magazine would have a section on mixed race or chess or tire swings and stolen bicycles? None.

Nor did the new Black magazines, *Obsidian* and *Broadside Press*, publish what could be written by O'Dwyer. What I did not do was contact my old Motown buddy, Ron Ivory, on the assumption that he was either ignorant or complicit.

I was sure my colleague would pause at a rest stop to rephrase his experiences, would keep in touch with himself by travelogue or a diary however pseudonymously.

Could Kevin have taken him over the bridge or through the tunnel to Canada? But was that too risky, with O'Dwyer's face in post offices, at border points?

I jumped at clues. Once I read a satire on "Ode on a Grecian

Urn," not by Keats, but by someone who had visited the Metropolitan Museum of Art's antiquities.

The satirist wrote:

> *Should I have been cracked,*
> *painstakingly glued together,*
> *Then I would be worth something.*

I hate breakage, marble deities with missing noses or arms, energetic warriors minus their heads, noble heads minus their torsos. Last summer I stood in the classical museum in Athens with body parts of my past surrounding me.

NOV. 2000+

Soon after the front-page article, I receive a forwarded letter from my old university in whose Bullpen I had grazed. The return address was J. Stewart, aka Noble O'Dwyer, with an assigned number and the prison.

"Anka," the letter begins, "are you still there? And, are you for me? I will always remember the comfort you brought me." It goes on:

> *Friends here in Oakland are chipping in for my bail. Are you "in the chips" now? More important, are you alive now? And still with that thick head of curly Greek hair? (If you've seen my coming-out photo you'll know I have eyebrow delineation, courtesy of the spot knocker, but am more like a cue ball.)*
>
> *It wasn't a good time to be betrayed—for that's what it was, after decades here. Whoever the betrayer, he was tempted by the reward money, I'm sure. But this is the wrong time and the wrong administration from whom to request clemency.*

(There are lines heavily blacked out. I'd forgotten about censorship in prison mail. Is O'Dwyer/Stewart commenting on the administration?)

I'm writing poetry again! I was underground all these years. What would I write when I was never anywhere very long: moldy ceilings, sour basements, uneven shades covering the windows?

But here I am very conscious of my isolated cell, my meals (I'm a veggie but that hasn't deterred the SPAM delivered to me on the lunch tray).

Write to me, my old Pen mate. Invest in me.

Yours,
Noble (or Ignoble)

THEN: Nightmare

After night class I am followed by my students to the Bullpen. They do not want the class to end. At last they leave. I take the elevator. The building is deserted. Then the dark walk to the university parking lot. I am the last car. I jump into it and take off.

More night, the street, the park, the black, black parking area behind the building. I rush to the dimly lit lobby, unlock the door to the stairway to the lower level. My hand trembles as I insert the key. I keep missing the slot.

I undress in the dark.

Someone has come in later than I. The front door upstairs closes quietly. I hear the stairwell door give and footsteps down the stairs. Only my apartment and the laundry room are on this level. (Both damp and dank.)

Is it O'Dwyer looking for refuge? I am about to open the door when I see the handle turning. I had remembered to put the chain on. And my car is in my designated space in the back. Someone knows I'm inside.

My phone line doesn't reach far. I stay in the shadow and dial the Palmer Park police.

"Someone's here," I tell them.

"It could be one of the officers making the rounds of the park," says the operator.

"No," I say. "It's one person, trying to get into my apartment."

"We'll contact the officers on patrol," I'm told.

I quietly put my feet pajamas on. If it's a rapist, let it be harder for him. If it's the police, I'm not here to seduce them.

There is a flashlight against my window, a knock on my door.

"Who?" I ask.

Clearly two.

"Palmer Park police," I'm told.

"How do I know?"

"Didn't you call, lady?"

"Do you see him?"

"No one here," I'm told.

"He must have gone out the back door," I say.

"Open the goddamned door!" I'm told.

It's the two officers.

The next morning I go into the back lot to retrieve my car. There are chalk marks on the tires as if the meter maid were timing me. But I'm in a space reserved only for the tenants.

THEN: Right After

"Kevin," I say, "I want to tell you something."

I hesitate.

"Yes?" he asked.

I can't.

Instead I say, "A report from Boiler Room."

THEN: Boiler Room

Boiler Room reads today.

I asked my great-granny about her life.

"Which life?" Granny asked. "I had lots of lives. I had the life of the child and the life of the mother and the life of the grandmother and, now, my last life."

"Granny," I said, "how did you live in hard times?"

"It was all hard times, sonny," she said.

"I mean the Depression hard times."

My great-granny laughed.

"We had a time. We always had a time. But the hardest of it was to get the rent money. So we had rent parties."

"What kind of parties, Granny?"

"Hell and heaven parties, sonny. Upstairs was heaven. We baked angel food cake. We had chicken breasts. We had mounds of mashed potatoes. We had sweet music upstairs. Downstairs was hell, where we served barbecue ribs, devil's food cake, whiskey, and Bessie Smith singing 'Touch My Spot.' And our friends and neighbors paid in coin to go to heaven or to hell. And then we had our rent for the month."

"The class applauded and Boiler Man bowed," I told Kevin.

"You're doing a good thing, Anka," he said. "Come over here and get a hug."

"Kevin," I said, "I don't go running for a hug."

"The mountain moves," said Kevin. He got up and tried to hug me in my desk chair. He lifted me from the chair. It was a good hug, and I hugged back and we stared at each other's lips. And our lips clung.

"No," said Kevin, "I can't do this. I beg your pardon."

He wiped his mouth and walked very fast down the corridor.

A few days passed. I never looked at Kevin's desk. Farmer was in and out, teaching or having meetings with students at his desk. He was quiet. Maybe it was the effect of the Winter Soldier Investigation. Or of new information in his life.

Farmer went to teach when I announced, "Another story from the night class."

Kevin swiveled around.

"It's from a recent Viet vet," I said. "The one who didn't have anyone to interview.

"'I interviewed myself,' he wrote. I said, 'What are you afraid of?'"

From Fearless Phil

    I answered,
    I fear. I fear everything.
    I fear nothing. I am Fearless Phil.
    I fear life ahead.
    I fear the past.
    I fear if I put a gun to my head,
    none of you will stop me.
    None of you will gather my belongings.

```
To send home
where I have not been in years.
I do not fear my going,
only that you will all depart
leaving my remains.
```

"Man," said Boiler Room, "you really said something!"
"That's deep," said another.
"But what'd he say?" asked a third.

"You're a fine teacher," said Kevin and turned his chair back to his desk.

A week passed and I called Kevin's name.

"Kevin," I asked, "should I worry about this student?"

"Which one? Boiler Room?"

"No. Fearless Phil."

"What has he done?"

"He interviewed himself again."

The Burying of Phil

```
I think of myself as newly buried.
I do not want to be alone.
Should we dig our graves together?
Should we dress formally
Or in old clothes,
the jacket split down the back,
in stocking feet,
to keep the line smooth?
We slumber
like nightshade or vampires
```

```
In our windowless home.
I do not want to linger
Any longer.
    Will you join me?
```

The class was silent.

"Something's a little off, man," said Boiler Room.

I told Kevin, "Fearless Phil rose. I was afraid he would attack Boiler Room. Instead, he just left the class."

"Boiler Room is right," said Kevin.

"But what do I do? Should I send him to the clinic for counseling? Or aren't they good enough? Should I send him to a doctor, a priest? Tell me, Kevin."

"I no longer hear confessions," said Kevin.

"Maybe you should!" I said.

Fearless Phil did not return for class the next week. Everyone noticed the empty chair that Phil had occupied near the door, coming in late, scurrying out early.

I did manage to obtain Phil's phone number from Student Affairs. He was home.

"Phil," I said, "we all missed you."

"They're all—we all—are a bunch of losers," said Phil.

"I would like you to come by my office for a conference," I said.

"You're gonna flunk me, make me a civilian?"

"Tomorrow evening, okay?"

I asked Kevin, "Can you hang around tomorrow night? I might need your services."

"No funny stuff," said Kevin.

At 7:00 p.m. I heard boots marching heavily down the corridor and a loud voice, "Company halt!"

Phil knocked and entered.

Kevin was on the phone, preoccupied.

"Please sit down, Phil," I said.

I borrowed a chair from O'Dwyer's deserted cubicle.

"You're a wonderful writer," I said.

Kevin hung up the phone, his back turned to us.

"I can only write about one thing," said Phil.

"Most writers have one large experience they write about over and over."

"This isn't an experience," said Phil, not looking at me, "because it doesn't go away."

"Like what?" I asked.

"I hear marching all the time, a whole troop. They never stop. Through the night I hear the tramping of feet."

He sat in the chair, marching in place, his feet pounding on the floor.

Kevin no longer pretended disinterest.

"Don't march yourself away," I said.

Phil rose, a big man, a big soldier.

"One thing I do all the time is weigh," said Phil. His hands became scales. "I am Justice. Right/wrong. My arms seesaw. Right/wrong. Where is she? Where is Justice in all this?"

He stood still; his arms stiffened, with alternate movements, right/wrong, up/down.

Minutes passed. Phil was still seesawing.

"Kevin," I said. "He's catatonic."

Kevin was there.

"Phil," says Kevin.

Kevin tried to stop the mechanically moving arms.

When Phil felt the pressure from Kevin, he fisted his hand.

"Watch out, Kevin!" I said.

"It's all right, Phil," Kevin told him. The arms slowed down and ceased.

"My son," said Father Kevin. "My wounded son."

Phil's body relaxed; his knees bent. Kevin held him upright. The hold became an embrace.

Phil cried against Kevin's chest. Kevin had his ready handkerchief.

"Am I crazy?" asked Phil. "I think I'm crazy."

"No," we both said at once. "You're not crazy."

"Then what's crazy?"

"You tell me," Kevin said.

"This war. The war's crazy."

"Fearless Phil," I said, "you are sane."

"And fearless," assured Kevin.

The next day I told Kevin, "I owe you."

Kevin said, "It was harder for me than you think. The power of it. With my own person I could forgive. My person was an embodiment of holy."

"Kevin," I said quietly. "I think you're holy."

He didn't hear, or did not want to.

"And I gave it up," he said. "Never to feel that way again. And who am I now?"

"A teacher and scholar."

"You know that isn't true. In the priesthood I knew who I was, and, here, on the outside, I'm a novitiate."

Fearless Phil dropped the class but visited periodically. He came down the corridor so quietly I only heard him when he knocked.

THEN: It Continues

I'm running slow. In fact I'm not running. I'm not even driving. I am sitting on my couch having cramps. My class is later. I call the Bullpen, Kevin's line.

"Kevin, would you do me a favor?"

"Depends," he says.

"A note on my door telling my students I'm canceling morning appointments."

"Anything wrong?"

"No," I say.

From the couch there is the nice parade of shoes between autumn and winter. No sandals, no open toed. Sneakers, was the wearer sneaking? Shoes with spikes on the soles to pierce the ice, though there's neither ice nor snow. Boots, noisy enough so I hear their approach. Every other pedestrian walks by. Puss 'n Boots stops. I see him trying to bend low enough to see inside. I skitter behind the couch. I wait. And wait. Nothing.

I won't call the police.

"Kevin," I phone again. "Someone's outside my window."

"I have a class, but I'll drop in after," says my hero.

It's an hour and a half before he gets there. No one's outside my window. Footprints have been printed over.

He rings, then he knocks. I'm still in my feet pajamas.

"No funny stuff, Anka," he warns.

I burst into tears, push him out the door, and slam it.

I cool down. Neither Kevin nor I say anything about it.

THEN: Berger and Boiler Room

"A Boiler Room story, boys," I said.

Both Farmer and Kevin are in their cubicles for office hours.

"Oh, boy," says Farmer, "but whatever happened to Berger?"

"First Boiler, then Berger," I said.

"The other way," insisted Farmer. "Berger, then Boiler."

"I received a form letter, signed by the chair. Did you?"

They nodded.

"Being considerate enough to give me notice that next year will be my last, and I may want to start applying elsewhere."

"Same sweet letter," said Kevin.

"More or less," said Farmer.

Farmer looked at the half-empty Bullpen.

"We're the last of the Mohicans," he said.

"Berger," reminded Kevin. "But you're not teaching him this semester, are you?"

"No," I said.

"I'm on the escalator at Hudson's Department Store. It's month-end sales, and I've found nothing on sale on the upper floors. I take the down escalator. There is Mr. Berger riding the up escalator, waving wildly at me!

" 'Our paths cross, Anka,' says Berger, 'only I'm up and away, and you're going down and out.' "

"Did he know what he was saying?" asked Kevin.

We were quiet.

"I've often wondered."

"Considering the circumstances, it's not so funny," said Farmer.

"Boiler Room," insisted Kevin.

Boiler Room's Second Story

Boiler Room asked if he could read his interview.

"I can't give out the name," he said. "It's confidential."

The class woo-hooed.

There's this favorite relative of mine, always affectionate, dressed up nice and not just for church. So I ask her, "How do you survive?"

"What you mean, boy?" she asks suspiciously.

"Just an assignment. How we get through the hard times. How we make out."

"Don't you know?" she teases me.

"I know you work at Pansy's Dress Shoppe out on Woodward and Eight Mile Road," I say.

"I do," she says. "But you think that pays the bills?"

Now I'm a grown man, right? I work at Ford's. I am taking a college class. And still I'm innocent.

"What pays the bills, Auntie?" I ask.

"Sonny," says my Auntie. "I'm a ho."

"Where at?" I ask.

"At Pansy's," she says. "It's a little bitty shop, customers poor, mostly Polish ladies and country folk. They like these cheap rayon dresses. But when they go to try them on, arms uplifted, no deodorant, wheee! I'm about to quit. As have others and they let the rest of the sales help go. It's only me on the floor and at the cash register. I open the place, I close it. And that's where I do my overtime."

"Auntie," I ask, "you charge the store for overtime?"

"I'm there, ain't I? The ho in the sto."

"Anybody know this?"

"I get my repeat customers," she says.

"And that's how you survive?"

"Survive and thrive," says Auntie.

"Don't tell my big sister," she makes me promise. "She don't know nothing about it."

So I say to Mama, "Should I interview Auntie and see how she survives?"

"No need," says my mama. "She's a ho in the sto."

The class screamed and applauded. Boiler Room was getting used to taking bows.

Boiler Room waited until the rest of the class left.

"Two things I want to ask you, ma'am," he said. "One is, can I use a word like *ho*? And how do you spell it? I can't find it in the dictionary."

"I don't know what they're learning in that class," said Farmer.

I insisted, "They are. They're learning."

"Like what?" asked my Pen mate. "That they're ethnic, can't spell, have whores in their families, are poor and wily?"

"Not like you, Farmer," I snapped. "So civilized, completing your dissertation, sending out resumes, getting out of debt, managing to be a family man—"

Farmer's face became red.

"That's enough," said Kevin. "Shame on you, Anka. As if we're all perfection here."

Farmer was mollified and I humiliated. But Kevin was curious.

"How *is* your dissertation going?"

That was exactly the wrong question for a graduate student. Of course, Farmer did not answer.

So the dissertation was not going well.

"How's your family?" I asked.

"Same old, same old," said Farmer.

So the family wasn't going well either.

He slammed his hand down on his desk.

"Elizabeth is pregnant," said Farmer.

"Wow," said Kevin and I.

"How come?" I asked.

"I fucked her, that's how come. I thought she couldn't conceive while she was nursing, and that's how come dumb," said Farmer.

He had been looking hunched over. The flair was gone.

I hesitate. I've been using a secret route to help my students. I put each young woman on a bus to Chicago, if possible with a friend, and provide her with an address. She will be safe, I'm assured, and will return by Greyhound the same day, if she can't afford to stay over. The students return, sore and pale but relieved, to resume their studies.

"Does she—do you—want it?" I ask.

"I'm not a baby killer," he said. "Not like you."

He opened the door, left it open, and took off.

"A baby killer?" Kevin asked me.

"Just one of my accomplishments."

But what, and how, did Farmer know?

NOW

I see in my document that the Detroit Police Department also knew. They were arresting ministers and rabbis who were providing information on the "route."

THEN: Just Checking

I have a moment of suspicion. The next time Fearless Phil visits me at night I'll ask.

"Where do you live, Phil?"

"East Detroit," he says.

"Do you take long walks or rides at night?" I ask.

"To where?" asks my student.

"The northwest section?"

"I don't have a passport to get there," says Phil.

I look puzzled and Phil says, "It's unknown territory. I don't like to go where I haven't been."

"But," I insist, "it's in the same city."

"No," says Phil. "Now, mostly, I take off my boots and sit where I know my life."

NOW, 2000+

Ex post facto, everybody is showing up in my life. Here I am corresponding with O'Dwyer. And Bernstein appears on my e-mail:

I know as I'm writing this that you're reading it in the same time. Time is what is strange in the land. When I first arrived, I'd see donkeys being led up the path near the Old City. I'd see horse-drawn carts coming into town from the kibbutzim. I'd see people point proudly at the IDF (Israel Defense Forces): Hayalenu, our soldiers. That time is past, dear Anka. And maybe it's just as well you never wanted to come here, even to visit me.

What am I reading? Disenchantment. From the man who had a bumper sticker, ISRAEL IS REAL, on his car because his students couldn't spell "Israel." Regardless of spelling, his bumper sticker would be blackened out when his car was parked near the university.

ANOTHER LETTER

It's never all grim, Anka. I don't want to give you the wrong idea. The land is funny!

My composition class in the English department was "The Self as Character." I have one older student. He's a former industrialist who made a mint and now wants to pay back the country. He says he wants to learn to teach English in development towns.

For "The Self as Character," Mr. Alberg wrote about his first year at the University of Lebanon.

"It was only a taxi ride away from Haifa," said Mr. Alberg. "My parents were worried because I had graduated from secondary school at fourteen. My Lebanese schoolmates soon discovered my age and religion. They teased me horribly.

"One day they tested me. 'Hey, Jewboy! We're going to a brothel. Are you a man or a mouse?'

"Actually I was a mouse.

" 'You first,' they insisted, and this woman came out, red-haired, zaftig, middle-aged. She took my hand and led me away.

" 'You're a boychik, nahon, right?' she asked. 'I have a secret also. I'm a Jewess.'

"She offered me tea and cookies and told me her life story and the time passed.

" 'Alberg!' the classmates yelled. 'What the hell's going on?'

"My hostess opened the door and called down, 'He's something!'

"I rejoined the others. I kept my mouth closed and head high. It was the end of the teasing."

Alberg is well thought of in the business world. There's some talk

*of his being appointed president of the University of the Negev! He'd
have to footnote me for teaching him composition.*

Laughingly yours,
Yaakov

NOW

There are cryptic recent notations on my file that I fail to deci-
pher. The dates seem consistent with Bernstein's e-mail. Wouldn't
that be illegal, for the FBI to monitor outside the land?

THEN, THE SEVENTIES

"Anka?" a familiar voice but with an accent.

"Yes?"

"This is your old Bullpen mate, the one you rejected when he
asked you to come to Israel with him."

"Jack Bernstein?"

"It's Yaakov now."

"Oh. Where are you?"

"Where you are."

"Here?"

"At the university Hillel organization, speaking on 'Today's
Israel.'"

I'm so surprised, I'm silent.

"It's an open lecture. You can come." A pause. "And then I'll
come to you."

It isn't a big turnout at the Hillel organization, not enough to
cover the cost of his round-trip fare. I almost don't recognize
Jack/Yaakov—bearded, thick head of hair, suntanned, casual,
easy in his body, easy in his report.

He responded to the questions, "Is it a capitalist state? Is it a socialist state?"

Bernstein said, "A mixed economy, with a large safety net. There are no beggars in the land, no homeless in the homeland, and the gap between rich and poor is the smallest among the developed nations."

The audience was impressed.

"It may not be Gan Eden, but, as a nation, we're only a few years old, so give us a chance."

Applause followed by modest refreshments, hot water, tea bags, and coffee cake.

"Ankale," he said after, "the rabbi put me up at his house to save money. Since it can't be my place, let it be yours."

I took him to my basement apartment on Palmer Park. Talkative Bernstein was quiet on the ride out. I drove and he rode nervously.

When I opened the door, he turned me toward him and kissed me. Not bad. All that army training and lecturing in Israel were good for him. His arms were muscled, his neck size bigger.

"I know I wrote to you about my feelings toward men, but I've waited for this," said Bernstein. "And I have feelings for you as well."

He began to undress as I was still standing there, the door half open.

"Take the key out of the door, Anka," he said. He grinned. "And I'll put my key in the lock."

He didn't wait for the bedroom. He bedded me right there on the couch. His pants were down. I was startled.

"What's the matter?" he asked.

"I never saw one like that before," I confessed. "I'm Greek and from Ohio." He slid out of his jockey shorts and I gasped. It was so bald.

"You mean circumcised?" asked Bernstein. "That's not possible. Everybody's circumcised. Think of all that nude Greek statuary—"

"But they weren't circumcised," I informed him.

We do it, sliding off the couch.

"This was just a snack. Next time, a real meal," said Bernstein.

He was on a tour of the campus Hillel clubs and then would return to the Promised Land.

"If I could only extract one promise from you," he said, "to think about joining me."

"I'll think," I said. What the hell?

The pillows had slid off the couch. I fluffed them and placed them back.

I had to be satisfied with the snack. For I never did get the whole meal.

The next day Kevin said, "Bernstein was here. It's in the campus paper."

"Right."

"You saw him?"

"I did."

"Why didn't he come by the Pen?"

"He mostly gave a talk and left."

"He didn't visit with you?"

"A minute."

"Is he the same or different?"

"Both."

"How does he look?" asked Kevin.

"For Bernstein, good."

"It's lonely in here," said Kevin. "O'Dwyer gone, Bernstein in the Holy Land, Farmer hardly around. The chickens have flown the coop, the horses the barn—"

"The bulls the pen."

"Except for you and me," said Kevin.

"I notice."

Kevin's look was full of longing.

"A few more months," he said.

Now *there's* the promised land.

THEN: In the Dark of the Park

I have tried to stay away from the apartment, but the city largely closes down in the evening. The library, just across from the university on Cass Avenue, shoos us away twenty minutes before locking the doors. The Institute of Arts, a block away on Woodward, has erratic hours. No evenings. Since Republicans were voted in, the galleries were voted out.

I give up roaming and return home. As soon as I enter, the phone rings.

"This is the Palmer Park station," says a booming voice.

"I didn't phone you," I said.

"Has anyone threatened you in the park or elsewhere?"

"Before, when I phoned you. But not lately. Anyway, I have nothing to do with the park," I said. "I don't even go into it."

"That's not quite accurate," the boomer chides me. "You were seen at various times, at the refreshment stand, at the bocce court, at the duck pond."

"Who's watching?" I ask.

"It's our duty," he says, "to protect the park."

I ask, "But who's protecting me from you?"

I am not dreaming. Not hallucinating. I hear drumming at night. By the glare of the streetlamp I see a corps of men dressed in green. They are drilling. What is this? The Drill of the Leprechauns?

There must be twenty out there, tall and slim, short and fat.

"It's war," I hear their drill sergeant yell. "One two three four, prepare for war."

I phone the police station again. They let it ring and ring.

Hello, reporting on suspicious goings-on. Sorry, no one home.

STILL THEN

"How's your night class going?" asked Kevin.

"Better and better," I told him. "Listen to this from a nurse's aide, named Florrie H. She worked in the psychiatric wards of prison."

"What's she doing in that class?" Kevin asked.

"She wants her RN. Working in the prison system, she learned that when you call a prisoner by name, he becomes a person."

"Litany of Names," a love poem to her incarcerated, listing given names, then surnames, and lastly, their nicknames: Weeny, B.O., Star, Ug (ly), Slime, and Shine.

Florrie ends her poem: "This is a love song for you / God didn't make no junk."

The class applauded Florrie H. wildly.

"'God didn't make no junk,'" Kevin repeated. "Wow!" He was packing up to leave.

"Wait! There's more."

"My dear Anka, there's always more," said Kevin.

There *was* more, the end-of-the-semester party. By now, it was a family class. We not only knew one another but the families as well. I asked permission to use the faculty lounge at night. With fanfare, before the gathered class, I unlocked the door. I had xeroxed photos of the group and decorated the walls with them and filled paper plates with pretzels and chips. Florrie, the poet of names, baked a chocolate cake with chocolate icing. Another proper matron brought a tablecloth and silverware for the seminar table.

"Anka," they said, "where do we go from here?"

"You are all named," I told them. "You can go anywhere."

I had carried in a box. The surprise: the class interviews, mimeographed and stapled, one for each student, with a title page, *City Smarts*.

"We're writers," said Boiler Room, finding his stories in the table of contents, "How We Survived the Depression" and "The Ho in the Sto," Thomas O'Connor, author.

Mr. O'Connor was nattily dressed, having left the factory early to stop off home and change into a suit.

We had a surprise visitor: Fearless Phil. He saw his two poems listed in the collection and stood for a photo with the class. The class signed their work for one another.

Phil signed his "Fearful Phil."

"Is that good or bad?" Boiler Room asked me about Phil's signature.

"It's an improvement," I said to Mr. O'Connor.

Someone brought a bottle of wine, but I could not allow it to be opened. I put on the coffee machine, and we had a fine old time, singing doo-wop. The janitor peered in, and Mr. O'Connor said, "Come in, man. Take this class and learn something."

INTO NOW

The letters and e-mails from Bernstein never stopped. Nor did the kvetching.

How were you prescient enough, Anka, to refuse my invitation? Slowly the economy has shifted from mixed to capitalist. Not so slowly the subsidized staples were deregulated. Fish, chicken, eggs, butter, milk are as costly as anywhere else. As for transportation, or phone, you're on your own.

Another letter:

Anka, the reason the social welfare is suspended is for defense. I'm not so happy thinking someone could sneak over the border and bomb me, believe me. But it's David and Goliath, and this time—alas!— we're Goliath.

And again:

This is for you. I am a Friend of Women in Black, Against the Occupation. I stand with them on Friday afternoons, and who's there in support? Madame Papandreou, wife of the president of Greece. (Or ex-wife.) She is wearing black and looking very serious about the Israeli-Palestinian situation. I thought you, from the Cradle of Democracy, would be pleased.

NOW AGAIN

Guess who fills my e-mail screen with daily bulletins, information on meetings, and weekly marches? The Gray Brigade. Myra, the aerobics instructor, wants to strengthen us bodily with yoga and martial arts so we'll be fit to fight during the coming election.

There is to be a demonstration at city hall, "Gray Brigade on Parade," and another minimarch, organized by Katy and Lois, in support of same-sex marriage, "Gay Gray Brigade." They are my mentors, my mothers, women in arms.

There are so many ways to contact people that the phone seems obsolete. I remember how it rang on each of our desks at the Bullpen. How seldom I received a call on my own phone in my Palmer Park apartment. Now I can fax, e-mail, call direct, write to an office or a home.

So it comes as a surprise when I receive snail mail, a real letter in my faculty mailbox.

"By now," it begins,

> you must be out of the Bullpen, perhaps in your own private office, with private secretary and private connecting number.
>
> By now, you probably have no memory of our little community or of your slow and silent Pen mate.
>
> I'll bring you up-to-date and then tell you why I'm writing. (Our old university gave me your forwarding address.)
>
> I did achieve separation from the Jesuits, on their terms. I did screw around immediately afterward (you were gone by then). And then I settled down—with Elizabeth Farmer.

NOW: Reacting to the Letter

Forty years later and still unbearable! The bitch! The fecund fucky bitch!

I had read a study of monkeys in cages. When they were neglected, their hearts developed lesions. One's heart does, indeed, break, even retroactively.

NOW: His Letter Continues

> You won't be surprised to learn Farmer left shortly after the second baby came. Strangely enough, he never agreed to a divorce. But Elizabeth wanted more than the domestic—she wanted to finish her doctorate. She remained in their house, rented out rooms to college babysitters, and there was no room for me.

Rather, there was a change, perhaps an annuity from her family. Something rather precipitous happened, or maybe people feel that way when they're thrown out. Elizabeth got through it all. And then began teaching composition at the Jesuit college in Jesu Parish where Holly was baptized. She went from being an adjunct to tenure track. And I was untethered.

Unlike Elizabeth, I never finished my dissertation. I became less interested in Flannery O'Connor, the sacred and fictional. The Kraut rightfully gave me notice. But he did something else.

He didn't summon me to his office. Instead, he came to the Bullpen. You know how socially awkward he is. He stood there a moment, at the door.

"Kevin," he said, "do something else. Not this, but something like it." He hesitated. "I wish you luck."

I had no idea what he was talking about.

And so I did something else and the same thing. A special program was set up by the university, Weekend College, to teach professionals the English they hadn't bothered to learn in college; writing briefs for lawyers, reports for doctors and accountants as well as speeches for labor leaders.

To my surprise, it was on our chairman's recommendation that I got the job. Despite the cuts in college budgets, our division sustained itself all these years.

Of course, Anka, I'm retired but still called upon as a consultant on setting up other weekend colleges.

I may be in your neighborhood.

THEN

Farmer was seldom in, not before or after class. It was the chair who wrote Kevin and me to inform us that Farmer had asked for leave in the middle of the semester, claiming "pressing family needs."

There had been substitutes for the classes taught by Bernstein and O'Dwyer. Now there would be Farmer to cover. Were we interested in doubling our load?

We were poor but not interested.

We were middissertation and had no time.

We were in our lives and couldn't add another's.

But, of course, we thought it over. Making money?

Hard to refuse.

By now I was in depression. One wearies of a dissertation. It seems to be the one book of your life.

So I read: Norman Mailer's *An American Dream*, John Rechy's *City of Night*, Donleavy's *The Ginger Man*, Leonard Cohen's *Beautiful Losers*. Instead of sex, I read Frank Harris's *My Life and Loves*. To the latter I masturbated before work and, if not too tired, after classes.

And, as the war dragged on and on, I added *Ramparts* to all the other antiwar newsletters and magazines I was reading.

Poets came to campus to declaim antiwar poetry: Denise Levertov, Louis Simpson, Galway Kinnell, whose straight hair fell into his eyes, and Robert Bly, who read his poems and leered at the young students.

"Something's wrong there. Something's very wrong," I said to a woman colleague about Bly.

"You're right," said my friend. "It's his big, fat—"

I was startled.

"Not just anatomy," she said, "Ego. Male ego."

We began thinking about women.

Florrie H., the nurse's aide from the night class, dropped into my office to tell me she had taken the side of her hand and knocked the jars off her spice rack.

"What for?" I asked.

"That's not who I am," she said. "I have another name."

The students were first to get it. The adjuncts next. Secretly, with a key they had hidden that opened the executive offices, the adjuncts spent the night xeroxing on the department's machine. By morning they had produced the first feminist academic magazine, *Moving In*. After asking her permission I contributed a short piece on my sometime-ago Lebanese writing student.

The Kraut never commented on it, probably never saw it, and certainly never would have understood it. These women had no love for Swinburne, Ruskin, or the famous literary tuberculars in Davos, Switzerland.

By chance, none of the staff of *Moving In* ever made tenure.

THEN, EARLY SEVENTIES: The Speak-Outs

There were speak-outs, with both students and faculty. Some of my students, who had confided in me when they learned of their pregnancies, asked me to go with them to the campus auditorium. I learned what it was like to be illegal though a citizen of the state—to be pregnant and unable to get an abortion. My students would be squeezing my hand as they spoke, as if they were still having cramps. It had been a nightmarish time for them, first pleading with friends to contribute to the expenses, then being left in a strange city and alone, hemorrhaging and feverish.

"Teach, just by being there, you take away the shame," they whispered.

I had visited some of my students at Harper Hospital's Psychiatric Ward. They were the ones who had had their babies but were crazed between class and baby, homework and diapers. It was my duty to take away the shame and blame.

And there were speak-outs by the law students, identifying the professor who had humiliated them in class, and also the young lawyers naming which firms had humiliated them afterward.

"But do it!" they said.

And there were speak-outs by the med students: what their classmates did to make the women fail, the jokes with the female cadavers, the biological jokes told by the professors.

"But do it!" they said. "Become premed, and go to med school!"

There were speak-outs on the Mall: Florrie escorted me and spoke out. She and other nurses told on doctors, whom they called "the boys."

"The boy is spoiled," they said. "He expects you only to cater, to obey, never interrupt, never initiate, and never take credit."

"But go for it!" the nurses ordered. "Be a professional, a nurse."

There were further speak-outs in the auditorium of business majors: from which business you could expect humiliation, which bosses touched you every time you passed their desks. As Florrie had named names in class and at the nurses' speak-out, so did these angry businesswomen. The perpetrators were not anonymous in their litany.

THEN: Reaction to Women's "Doing it"

There have been meetings all over campus. Women's rights, they're called. What about their violating the rights of the doctors, lawyers, and businessmen?

In indignation,

Edgar Miller, Editor,

Right Thinking

I had no one left in the Bullpen to tell. I was wary of Kevin's disagreement or disapproval. I could not engage in casual conversation about what I had heard.

If I wrote Bernstein, he wouldn't get it. He had written, "Anka, Israel is ten years behind the States."

What could I do with all this added information? Continue to teach, go to meetings, and listen to music.

I listened to the Beatles and the Byrds and Canned Heat and, best of all, Judy Collins's *In My Life*.

I heard the Jefferson Airplane, Donovan, Country Joe and the Fish, the Grateful Dead, Janis Joplin, and Crosby, Stills and Nash, and Dylan's *Bringing It All Back Home*, *Highway 61 Revisited*, and *Blonde on Blonde*.

None of the instructors could have resisted Dylan. We even tried to turn him academic, and one of us gave the Instructors' Lecture Series, in the faculty lounge, on an exegesis of his lyrics.

Kevin was somewhere else. I bumped into him when I went to the John Coltrane concert, Coltrane playing from *A Love Supreme*. I saw Kevin again at a Miles Davis concert where Miles was playing from *Bitches Brew*.

Kevin was by himself at Coltrane. And, to my hurt surprise, with Elizabeth Farmer at the Davis concert. What kind of family emergency did Farmer mean?

I don't think about my heart. I've never been to a cardiologist. But, I swear, my heart was sore. Right there, left side. Paining. Longing yet trying to avoid him.

Because we were in the city, of course I heard Aretha Franklin, "I Never Loved a Man (The Way I Love You)" and *Lady Soul*.

Motown people lived near me, on the Northwest Side of town, where I once saw the sweet tenor Marvin Gaye when I drove by a Carvel ice cream parlor. I sat in my car for a moment to watch him lick that cone. I sang his "Sandman" until I reached the parking lot behind my apartment building on Seven Mile Road.

EARLY SEVENTIES: Still a Motowner

Motown was at 2648 W. Grand Boulevard. The Motowners hung out at the art deco house on Outer Drive. The Four Tops would be coming down the stairs and driving off in their fine cars.

Mr. O'Connor, "Boiler Room," dropped by one evening at my office. He had on his suit.

"Dr. Anka," he said, "some of us are going to the Flame Show Bar. Want to join?"

I joined.

"This town is Hitsville," said Mr. O'Connor. "And this bar is the center of it."

This was a black-and-tan bar. One of the musicians, on keyboard, was white. Mr. O'Connor went up to talk to him between numbers.

"His name is Moe," he said. "He's been playing around for a while."

Moe seemed startled to see me as I danced by.

Does he know me from somewhere?

Another evening, after one of my night classes, Mr. O'Connor came by again. "Professor," he said, "ready for a spin at the Greystone Ballroom?"

So, indeed, we spun and spanned the distance between us of rank and color.

"There he is," Mr. O'Connor pointed. "Moe again."

Moe sees O'Connor and shows off fancy fingering on the keys.

"Listen to his chords," said O'Connor. "It's hard to believe he's white."

At the Greystone we danced smooth and slippery. This was sinuous and dangerous. This was the Motown "styling," a strut, clapped hands, turning around. One might never again wish to do a circle dance, the hora or polka. (Not even "The Blonde Secretary's Polka," popular on Detroit radio.)

Moe talked to O'Connor but not to me. Then why did he keep staring? Was it because we were a mixed couple, Black and white? But Moe was in a mixed-race band. So what was so surprising?

Smokey Robinson was writing for everybody, the Miracles, the Marvelettes, the Temptations. I suppose I could have been happy. I should have been happy. But I wasn't.

If I had smoked I would have. If I had coked I would have. If I could have found somebody to fuck, I would have.

I heard Mothers of Invention. Sly and the Family Stone, and *The Best of Steppenwolf*. I thought I was too old for jealousy and heartbreak and boredom and too young to tire of the war.

Both Kevin and I had added Farmer's classes to our load and almost never saw each other after that. I took time off, bleary eyed though I was, for the film *2001: A Space Odyssey*. Kevin was there with Elizabeth Farmer, Elizabeth hanging on his arm for support. Is she limping? Is she injured? No, she's just clinging.

What a rotten mother leaving Holly alone!

Oh, fickle Aphrodite! All that time and energy I put into the Bullpen.

To avoid encountering them at night, I went to a noon showing, in the suburbs, of *Bonnie and Clyde*.

I begin to dream that I'm screwing everybody I ever met: Mr. O'Connor, skinny Farmer. It's disgusting—from the Kraut to Mr. Berger. No Kevin. Not allowed.

Athena, like yours, my head is heavy with thought. Let me out of this decade, out of this city, out of my dissertation! Away from my sore heart.

THEN: The Surprise Visitor

Who phones me at my extension in the Bullpen. (I'm almost the only one there these days.) Professor Ronald Ivory. He's on my floor in the English department.

He opens the Pen door. He looks around.

"A bomb fell here," he says.

Empty desks, discarded paper and books.

"First," I say, "kiss-kiss, hug-hug."

We do.

"Are you looking for O'Dwyer?" I whisper.

"Who isn't?" he asks in his deep baritone. "Came to visit a few friends from the dark side," he says. "And I've got a buddy playing at Baker's Bar."

He almost doesn't invite me!

"You can't go there alone," I say.

"Who's alone?" he asks me.

So, there they are, Ron's friends, the Funk Brothers, brilliant and drunk and doped out.

"Moe!" says Ron to the white guy on keyboard.

"Too long," says Moe. "I'll die so you'll come and see me at my wake."

It's bar dark in here except for the photo lights on the walls, decorated with the album covers put out by Motown. They're all backed by the Funk Brothers. I recognize the Four Tops, Marvin Gaye, the Marvelettes, Martha and the Vandellas.

I'm chivalrously seated at a table not far from the musicians, who have already put in a full day at the Motown studio before doing sets at Baker's.

I'm self-conscious and cover myself with my arms. I'm the only white except for the piano player. Ron's hardly with me. He shares the piano bench with Moe a good part of the evening. At the break he brings Moe over to the table.

"My Greek goddess," says Ron. "Meet Moe the Most."

"Is she an authentic Greek goddess?" asks the Most.

"Is the Parthenon authentic?" asks Ron.

"There are a lot of Greek goddesses around," says Moe, "and they're not all authentic."

"I'm not Greek," I correct. "I'm Hellenic."

"If you say so," Moe tells me.

He's bald in the front and has a long ponytail down the back. It's sort of Chinese looking. Indeed, he's wearing a Chinese shirt with frogs that button.

"Did you play at the Flame?" I ask.

"I did," says Moe.

"And at the Paradise?"

"That too. And Millie's Chit Chat Lounge on Twelfth Street."

That one I didn't know.

"You live in the city?" I ask.

"No. I travel."

Ron interrupts. "Time to travel now," he warns. "Your break is over." He turns to me. "Anka, love of my life, I'm gonna be hanging around until they wrap up. Let me get you home."

"I don't want to interrupt anything," I say.

Why should I go home to the basement?

"No trouble," says Ron. "You're a hop and skip away."

"Here are my keys," says the Most. "Take my car."

"Berry Gordy must be proud of the Funk Brothers," I say in the car.

"No," says Ron. "He even hates their name. Wanted them called the Soul Brothers."

"But they've made all those albums. Aren't they famous?"

"They're anonymous, girl," says Ron. "It's easier to exploit them that way."

The treatment of his friends angers him. But he manages to kiss me as he deposits me at my door.

THEN AND CRANKY

It makes me dreadfully lonely to be in the Bullpen. Am I now the keeper of the Bullpen Award Board, the antiwar periodicals on the empty shelves? The Greek sailor's cap that's become dusty? The research on Flannery O'Connor in the file cabinet? Am I the only one with memory?

NOV. 2000+: Disenchantment in the Enchanted Land

They're building a fence that's snaking through the land, mostly Palestinian, to safeguard us. Most of us don't see that fence. We only do "Jewish things," meet with fellow Jews at the café, read the Jewish press, or stay at home with friends and family. Curious, as I always am, I went to take a look.

Anka, it is a towering barricade with guard turrets and guns poking out at the populace, splitting Palestinian towns in half.

There were makeshift steps at a division in the wall so the townspeople could get to the other side, to family, the grocery, their fields.

I saw old people with canes shakily maneuvering the stairs.

Am I complicit in this?

Yaakov

NOV. 2000+

"I'm in the hood," says a deep voice, slightly Irish in lilt.

I'm in my office.

"How close?" I ask.

I hear a knock on the door. Kevin is standing there with his cell phone.

We close the office door. We look askance at each other, too shy to look head-on. He's older, fleshier, a bit stooped, hair gray.

I'm older, fleshier, gray-streaked hair.

We instantly become much handsomer.

I hold out my right arm to shake hands. He takes the arm and draws me to him. He kisses my hand. Then leans over me. I raise my face. The sun shines on it.

"'Sugar Pie, Honey Bunch,'" he says.

"'Can't help myself,'" say I for the Four Tops.

I put a note on my door regretfully dismissing my office hours.

As I drive my car Kevin is holding on to my hand, and I steer from side to side on the road.

I park in the driveway of my little house.

"Are you hungry?" I ask.

"Yes!" he says.

We hold each other, slipping and climbing the stairs to the bedroom. It's darkening early when I pull down the satin comforter.

"Hurry," says Kevin. "I've waited so long!"

When I see my beautiful Bullpenner, I say, "Oh, that looks right!"

"My penis?"

"Yes."

"Well, that's good," he says.

We kiss, we kiss, and soon his mushroom penetrates the damp soil. Again and again. I will never let him move out of me.

Or move out.

We're up all night.

"There's something about this relationship," I say, "that precludes sleep."

In the early morning we begin to talk.

"Have you heard from O'Dwyer?" asks Kevin.

"Yes," I say.

"Have you heard from Farmer?" I ask him.

"No," he says, "curiously."

"I saw Ron more than once coming to hear music in Motown. He had a favorite musician . . ."

"Oh," says Kevin.

"Right," I say.

"Hear from Bernstein?" he asks.

"I have, and I'm worried," I tell him.

It seems we're still stuck in the Bullpen.

We can't separate so he comes to the college with me. I leave him in my office, but he asks his way to my classroom. He knocks on the door.

"May I sit in?" he asks the class.

They look at me, at him. We both have chapped lips and cheeks. My face is scratched from his unshaven face. They know.

"Sit in!" they invite.

I was wrong about them. I love them.

MORE NOW, 2000+

We want to do everything. We talk with our mouths full. We kiss and remember something we want to ask. We can't be silent, yet we cannot say everything all at once.

We have the Bullpen conversation.

"So you heard from O'Dwyer?" says Kevin.

"Yes."

"And you heard from Bernstein."

"I did."

"How are they?"

"One was a Weatherman, and the other may want to be," I say.

STILL NOW

"Dear Anka," writes Bernstein,

> We beat our chests during the High Holy Days and say, "I'm guilty,"
> al cheyt. I am *guilty that I lived a normal life when, on the other*
> *side of the mercury, the mirror, life has shattered.*

"Kevin, my dearest, what do we do?"

"We go to them," says Kevin.

"Yaakov," I e-mail, "we're coming to you. We'll rent a car at the airport, drive down to the Be'er Sheva and be there."

As is his wont he replies immediately.

"Beloveds," he writes,

It may not be so easy for you. Files are shared between the two states.
If you have a political past, they can turn you right around. It
happened to friends of mine, including that wonderful singer, the
redhead, who became a Rabbi for Human Rights and was deported
on the next plane. O'Dwyer's situation is seriously immediate. Be
with him.

He pressed SEND.

Another SEND:

No doubt, my e-mails are being monitored. How convenient for
someone who wants to know where we are and when we gather.

Spring break, we fly to San Francisco. O'Dwyer is out on bail.
He sits like a guru in his Oakland living room, crowded with loving friends and housemates. Two friends are holding a hand each.
His head is bald or shaven and the lamp behind gives him an
aura.

"O'Dwyer!" we say.

He rises and hugs us tightly.

"O'Dwyer?" he says. "I've been someone else for so long, I don't
know if by any other name I would be as sweet. My trial's coming
up. Will you stay?"

"Yes," we both say.

"Kevin," asks Jerry/O'Dwyer, "will you be a character witness?"

"I'll swear that you're a character," teases Kevin.

He introduces us as "friends from a normal life."

O'Dwyer's housemates are colleagues in the healing professions: acupuncturists, aromatherapists, reflexologists, yoga teachers. They know him as Jerry.

"I haven't known an English professor in a long time," he tells us. "With my new identity, I went back to school, got my high school equivalency, then on to acupuncture school. I couldn't use any of the university degrees I had received in my former, my normal life."

He was always soft-spoken, quiet. He still is, but he isn't wretchedly questioning everything. Despite being caught, he's calm.

"Who turned you in?" I whisper.

"I don't want to know," says O'Dwyer.

"How was the jail where they held you?" asks Kevin.

"It was kind of a Bullpen, only more crowded," says O'Dwyer.

His neighbors come in to welcome him home. It's a blue-collar community, mainly African American.

O'Dwyer introduces and praises them.

"They were the ones, during the earthquake, that went onto the damaged bridges to do rescue work. They themselves got nothing out of it."

"Wrong, Jerry," says a neighbor. "We did God's work, and God repaid us."

"Who turned you in, bro?" asks another neighbor.

"It was 'cause of the picket line," says the first, the one who does God's work.

O'Dwyer explains to us, "A new supermarket opened whose owners were from Texas. You can imagine how Texans felt about the strong union that was already recognized. Their aim was to break the workers by breaking the union."

"We couldn't get a new contract," says a neighbor. "All the other supermarkets reneged. We set up a picket line and there was old Whitey picketing with us. You might say he stood there for all to see, bald and white and shiny."

"It must have been a scab, a union buster, that busted him," says another neighbor.

"Or a friend," says yet another, "for the old do-re-mi."

The door was unlocked, but there was a knock and a ring.

"Sounds like a guy who's wearing a belt and suspenders," says a neighbor.

In a way it is. It's properly attired Ron Ivory, with belt and suspenders. He's rounder all these decades later. He was balding when we knew him, but he's gone total, the way O'Dwyer has.

NOW AND THEN

What made Ron rounder, balder, more conservative with suspenders and belt?

Experience. How can you express care, if not love, for your students or colleagues? You eat together. It may be dangerous to invite one or another to your home, so you make arrangements with a chef at a nearby gourmet restaurant, after class, every other Friday. You order good liquors, choice appetizers, and a simple but elegant meal, likely fish, plus a careful dessert. Not so many calories that one's eyes light up.

One monitors gestures, portions, measures the feelings poured out—one-fourth cup, half a cup . . . Appearance was all—private and public.

But inside, Motown raged. Inside, Hitsville hit. The inside person strutted, twirled, clapped.

The outside person enjoyed propriety and trusted friends. Once those were gained, Ron never again applied for or accepted offers from other universities. He was in demand, as were his writings: an article now and then, a careful book—not too controversial—and the programs he planned for his university were open to, acceptable by, all. His MO was "cautious." But not now.

NOW

The neighbors stare at this unfamiliar Black visitor.

"Noble!" says Ron.

"My God, Ron!" says O'Dwyer.

They race to each other's arms, kissing long and deeply.

A neighbor whistles. Another begins fanning her face with a church fan.

"That ain't nice," the church lady whispers.

"Two guys ain't nice," says another.

"Vanilla and chocolate besides," says the church lady.

The neighbors leave. We remain in the living room while the housemates retire upstairs. It's the Bullpen again.

"Where's Bernstein?" asks Ron, when he and O'Dwyer finally disentangle.

"The Holy Land," says Kevin.

"Getting himself in trouble," I say.

"And Farmer? What happened to him and the missus?" asks O'Dwyer.

"They bought their separate farms," says Kevin.

"Really?" asks Ron.

"In a manner of speaking," says Kevin. "Our office mates have a way of disappearing."

"Farmer went underground?" asks O'Dwyer.

"No," says Ron. "He came east to see me a few times."

"What about?" asks O'Dwyer.

"Lots of reminiscing. He was looking for work, he said. Did we have anything? Not likely. He hadn't finished his dissertation and never published."

"He wouldn't get a recommendation from the chair, leaving in the middle of the semester." I am still annoyed.

"What did you guys talk about?" Kevin wants to know.

"About you, among other things, the priestly abductor who stole his wife away from him," says Ron.

"Actually not," says Kevin.

"And he wondered how Anka was. Did she write any more fiction? *And* O'Dwyer. Did his life work out? It was neighborly concern of one Bullpenner for another."

"Was Farmer ever concerned about anything?" I ask.

"A lot about himself," says Kevin. "Not the wife or the kids, for sure."

"Nor academia," I add.

"I wrote to Anka, but, Ron, how did you know to come to Oakland?" O'Dwyer asks.

"I learned to read hidden news items," says Ron. "African Americans read that way. Words are black and white, but information is seldom black. Back section, bottom of the page, is where I thought I'd find clues. But you made a bigger spread than that."

"Who else would be looking for you?" I ask.

"The people who found me," says O'Dwyer. "Hide-and-Seek was over."

We're quiet.

"Wait," says O'Dwyer, "someone's not here." He smiles, a lovely smile. "Mr. Berger!"

"Tell a Mr. Berger story," my Pen mates demand.

"Remember," I said, "when I gave him a C, changed to a C plus and he reported me to the Kraut? Then next semester I open the campus paper, and there's a letter signed by Berger with the Greek letters of his frat attached."

All these years later, the letter still irritated me so that I could recite it by heart:

Watch out for certain teachers. Unfairness is their motto.
    Let me warn students against Anka Pappas of the English

department, un-American, as you can tell from her name. Avoid her like the plague. If you catch what she's got you'll break out into a rash!

> Warningly yours,
> Alvin Berger, Phi Delta Phi

The Bullpen laughs. "'Avoid her like the plague,'" says O'Dwyer. "Or you'll catch what she's got!"

"And break out in a rash!" says Ron.

"It's not as funny as 'It was a warm genital evening,'" says O'Dwyer.

"Or 'A hairy man climbed into Her Ladyship's cockpit,'" says Ron.

"Mustached," corrected Kevin.

I said, "Think of what harm a nutto kid can do!"

"Ah," says Kevin. "And are you not, my good O'Dwyer, a bit of a nutto kid?"

"A bit," admits O'Dwyer. "But adults aren't so great either. I've had decades of them, after going incognito into the world, hitching, staying in motels, rooming houses, taking every job. I know adults everywhere, and fifty percent aren't so grown up."

"How did you do it, Noble?" asks Ron. "How did you blow up the ROTC station?"

O'Dwyer thinks about whether or not to answer.

"The day after the whole business with the Detroit police, I placed a paper bag outside of the ROTC office. It contained an alarm clock, battery, electric blasting cap, plastic bag filled with gasoline and explosives."

"It blew up," I said. "I was in my office on campus."

"I'll tell you the truth, I was surprised myself," said O'Dwyer. "I was never good at that sort of stuff, making firecrackers with my brother. Mine always fizzled."

"This one didn't fizzle," I said.

"Why did you move around so much, love?" asks Ron. "I never knew when I would hear from you. And I was hesitant, for both our sakes, on whether to track you down."

"It wouldn't have been easy, Ron. I wasn't where anybody who had known me would expect to find me."

How sad to have to obliterate the data of one's life.

"On the other hand, my photograph was in police stations, post offices, and all federal buildings," said O'Dwyer. "If you had to renew your driver's license or buy postage or apply for a passport, there I was staring out at you, although younger and still with hair. So I wore a wig and a mustache, like the hairy man in Berger's story."

He smiles, and we laugh sadly.

"I changed my lifestyle. I renounced the world of literature. I renounced myself. But I guess, in the end, it didn't help."

"You got out on bail," said Kevin.

"Can you believe it?" O'Dwyer says, and his eyes tear. "My housemates and neighbors borrowed ninety-five thousand dollars on their houses for bail. Talk of goodness."

"What do you face?" asks Kevin.

"I face a maximum sentence of five years in jail and a one-thousand-dollar fine on the federal bombing conspiracy charge and ten years in jail and a ten-thousand-dollar fine on a federal charge of possession of an unregistered destructive device. I face state charges from a 1969 antiwar demonstration. I also had a gun, not registered to me, that I was given for my protection."

Ron looks away.

We're all silent.

"It was in my Red Squad files," I tell them. "That I was there when the building was bombed."

"Red Squad? Files?" ask the Bullpenners.

"My Detroit Police Department files of the sixties, early seventies," I say.

"The same police that framed me?" asks O'Dwyer.

"The same old," I say. "Or a group within that department that called itself the Red Squad. They tracked, or paid others to sniff out our trail of lurid, criminal activities."

"Do they have files on me?" Ron asks worriedly.

"I don't know, dear," I say. "Maybe not. I think you left before it all began. You can petition them through Freedom of Information and get hold of your files."

"FOIA," explains O'Dwyer—he pronounces it "foya"—"is a citizen's right to petition for documents."

"Is it still that way?" asked Kevin.

"No," says O'Dwyer, who knows about these things, "they're stuck in bureaucracy again."

"Is that what you did?" Ron asked me. "You sent away for them?"

"No," I told him. "Someone did it to or for me. They were just there on my doorstep one day."

"Your Red Squad was lying out there in the open?" asks Ron.

"Open and wet," I said.

"How weird," says O'Dwyer.

"What will you do with them?" Ron wants to know.

(Is he worried that they—if the Red Squad still exists or another like it—will tell his secrets to his university?)

"I don't know yet," I said.

"You don't have the original?" Ron is still anxious.

"No," I said. "Somewhere in that building in Greektown, or elsewhere, is the original."

I turn to O'Dwyer. "What will happen to you, dear friend?" I ask. "Do you know?"

"No, I don't know," says O'Dwyer.

Ron embraces him. "We've only just been reunited with you. We won't let anyone take you from us again."

THEN, THE SEVENTIES

I had just moved to an assistant professorship in Ohio when I received the *English Department Alumni News.*

It read:

Mr. Alvin Berger, class of '69, has been appointed to an executive position in the Department of Parks. There he will use the many skills he gained at the university. He is editor in chief of the *Park Press.*

Park news, I chortled:

> *Where is Maintenance*
> *To mow the grass,*
> *To remove the glass*
> *from the sandbox?*
> *Who counts the nesting birds?*
> *Who cleans the dog turds,*
> *or informs me which teeter-totters*
> *are teetering and which tottering?*
> *Which swings are creaking*
> *and slides rusting?*
> *Who will get rid of the nasty black squirrels*
> *without poisoning the boys and the girr-uls?*

I could riff on such a subject forever.

How strange that I could hear the military commands as the uniformed men marched. They were training in the picnic grounds. Who were they? Minutemen? Vigilantes?

What were they guarding? The barbecue pit, the bocce field, the molting ducks?

And why was a squad of park people training for war?

NOW: Oakland

O'Dwyer is fading. Ron has his arm around him and is watching anxiously.

"Anka!" Ron calls out. "I'm hungry. You promised another Berger."

"Berger's at the end of the story, so hold your appetite," I warn Ron.

"It was during the strike that these strange people came back into my life."

"What strike?" asks O'Dwyer.

"What strange people?" asks Ron.

"The strike where we took on the university," I say.

"Where was I?" asks Kevin. "Wasn't I there?"

"You were brooding over your life," I say meanly.

"Oh," says Kevin.

THEN: Striking Back

We had organized a unit of the American Federation of Teachers. I was on the bargaining committee, except the university wouldn't bargain. Remember their hard-nosed attorney who wouldn't give O'Dwyer a break? She didn't give us one either.

And the AFT couldn't offer us advice. Its experience was in public schools, not universities.

"What should we do?" we asked one another.

A custodian cleaning the hall heard us.

"Go to Solidarity House," he said. "They'll show you the tactics."

Solidarity House was the headquarters of the United Auto Workers.

"Strike the plant," they advised us.

That meant we had to convince all the other unions to show support. And we struck the plant together.

We met on the plaza in front of the Walter Reuther Labor Archives.

NOW

"If only I'd been there!" said O'Dwyer.

"You would have been arrested forty years earlier," Ron reminds him.

THE CAMPUS STRIKE

We had issues to bring to the table: cost-of-living increases, public disclosure of salaries, a role for the faculty in salary and promotion. No response from the administration. We were forced to call a strike.

Our chairman, old Sour Kraut, filled our metal mailboxes with warnings: "The professorial classes are not workers, but if you persist in behaving as such, you will be treated as workers with a time clock for punching in when you arrive and punching out when you leave."

"Hiss! Boo!" say my Bullpenners.

We were nervous. Could we exercise discipline over the various points of view? It wasn't exactly Sparta versus Athens, but could we inexperienced organizers maintain control?

Then the head of the custodial union mounted the platform

we had built. The custodial union consisted of Black employees only. The spokesman was dressed for this solemn occasion in white shirt and dark suit. I was up close and could see that he had just been barbered. There were flecks of hair on his starched collar.

"Brothers and sisters," he said into the mike, "the union is with you. We want to show support. We figured you're worrying about the strike lasting and you about to lose your health insurance. The brothers voted to help make your payments during the time you're on the picket line."

I was so moved, but who broke the spell? Farmer, the very Farmer in the Dell.

"What was he doing there?"
"On campus?"

"Congratulations for striking," he said, shaking our hands up and down the line. He paused in front of me. "You've got balls, Anka."

"That's news to me."

I knew he was a show-off, but what was he showing off? Then there was this other guy. I'd seen him in his green elf uniform and boots, training in the park.

"She's hallucinating."

. . .

And harassing me. Lobschultz. He belonged to one of those Far Right groups, Break Up, and he's yelling through his bullhorn:"It's illegal for public servants to strike. You teachers get back in the classroom where you belong ."

He's got it wrong and this academic lineup is quick to correct him.

"It's legal," said Sol Fineman from education. "We're the American Federation of Teachers. They're our recognized bargaining agent."

Old Lobotomy wasn't listening. "You're a Communist front," he accused, "and your purpose is to inflame the student body."

"Inaccurate!" yelled an offended historian. "We're socialists." And Romance Languages said, "Maybe you, but some of us are Trots." And that fat conventional sociology prof said, "No, we're Democrats!"

And Old Lob was messing with the picket line, congratulating the scabs who broke through and shaking their hands. To their credit, they had the sense to be embarrassed.

We were rescued from anarchy by the custodians, who called campus police. They hustled the worm off, but, before they forced him into the patrol car, he yelled, "Anka, I know your address."

"Did he, Anka?" asks Kevin.

"Not to worry, my dear," I tell him. "We won the strike and that was the last I heard from him."

"How did winning the strike affect you, my love?" asks my guy.

"I never had to ingratiate myself again."

"With whom?" asks Kevin.

"Not with youm," I tease. "Youm was not available. With the Kraut."

"Yech," my Bullpenners say. Kevin turns away.

"Kevin," I remind him, "did I 'yech' you and Elizabeth?"

"Mrs. Farmer?" The others "yech" it.

"The Kraut loved to be amused," I say, "but didn't know if it was appropriate for the chairman to show levity. I assured him it was appropriate, and we laughed about freshman papers, the spoonerisms, malapropisms."

Kevin is looking unconvinced.

"Oh, stop it," I say. "You act as if we were lap dancing."

Kevin is even more shocked.

"The Berger part, class. Pay attention!" I say. "Whom did I see hiding in the bushes, because he saw himself as Boss of the Bushes, an underling to Lobschultz. Your very own Mr. Berger, with his stupid little notebook and sharpened little pencil."

I sum up, "This leads to four questions. What was Farmer doing at the strike? What was Lobschultz up to? Why was Mr. Berger in the bushes? And why was this put into my files by the Red Squad?"

"Shades of Red," says O'Dwyer. "Pink like the water after bleeding gums, Red as a shaving cut, Scarlett as O'Hara." He yawned. "Does this have anything to do with me?" he asks, "aside from my being Red Red? I'm only interested in what has to do with me now."

"I don't know," I say. "But there are obliterated names in my file—I think the informer's. I suspect they cross-index connections."

"And the other Bullpenners?" Ron asks.

"Kevin may have his own file—taking objectors across the border or ordering antiwar magazines. But he's not in mine. O'Dwyer and Bernstein *are*. And the strike—everybody—the picket line, the strike committee, and even the custodial union!"

"The strike wasn't antiwar," says Kevin. "So why?"

"Makes you wonder what the spying is all about," I say.

"Besides that, friends," I end, as O'Dwyer sleeps sitting up, "we share one thing. We've each kept a secret from the others."

THEN: The Fourth Estate

Despite its being illegal to strike, the faculty went out on line. They were an unseemly bunch, shouting and singing!

This does not bode well for the independence of the administration under the pressure of a radical union. Mark my words.

Edgar Miller, Editor
Right Thinking

NOW: Still Talking

If television could tell you anything, we'd all be learned. But we did learn one thing. The new head of FEMA, the organization to handle disaster and its aftermath, was chosen.

"Good God and Goddess!" I shriek.

It's Lobschultz, "chosen because of his vast experience with the great outdoors, including the park industry." Industry? Grass, glass, birds, and turds?

And perhaps, among his achievements, was militarizing the park personnel, preparing them for a secret war?

VERY NOW

Since this has been a Pen meeting, it wasn't a surprise when we returned to our motel room and I opened my laptop, to find an e-mail from Bernstein.

Dearest Friends,

I've learned from your notes, cryptic but clear, that the Bullpen is in session. I am the only one out of the picture, so to say. My picture, to continue the metaphor, is very focused. It's like a missile was just landed in Be'er Sheva. Who was here but our very own Bullpenner. I've been in his focus a long time now, it occurs to me. Farmer, I mean. Always out to get me. (Do attest to my not being paranoid!) Did you know he is a J. Edgar Hooverite? Did you suspect he was in their employ? He was such a nebbish in the Pen, but now, in the FBI, he does wield power. He is here to bring pressure on behalf of the American government for my deportation. It's something with that bombing incident on campus long ago, I believe. I'm confused. Wasn't I in the Negev then? But as Farmer questions me, his English sounds foreign to me, so I hesitate as if to translate it. Or am I, as always, the foreigner to him? And now I am in his clutches!

The state of Israel is not so happy with me either. (Remember my ISRAEL IS REAL bumper sticker? It's getting too real.) I was reminded by the Ministry of the Interior that I, as an immigrant, an aliyah, had been given every advantage—from housing, tax-free loans on a car, to the right to import appliances also tax free. And how do I repay the state? By criticizing state policy. They know where I've been: at the peace rally in Rabin Square, at the Friday afternoons Women in Black, watching at the checkpoints. Now, they want me to repay them for the loans.

They will likely succumb to the feds, the G-men, to Eliot Ness of old. To Farmer, who is inexplicably one of them!

Whatever you do, don't exile me from the Bullpen.

Bernstein

Kevin is leaning over my shoulder.

"Farmer!" he says.

"For how long?" I ask Kevin.

"Maybe since he left, midsemester."

"But what about wife and child and child-on-the-way?" I ask.

"He knew I'd be responsible," says Kevin. "The more fool I!"

"Why, my dearest dear?"

"I fear I may have been used," says my darling boy, lifting me from the chair so he can lower his head to mine.

"By whom?"

"Not 'youm,'" he teases momentarily. "Maybe by them all."

I still don't get it.

"After I eased things for her," he says, "and, truthfully, she eased things for me also, there was an influx of money. She had no more need of me."

"They were sharing the loot? The *schmutz*?" I ask. "But who was the informer, the Red Squad agent?"

"He, but she was smarter than the Farmer," Kevin says. "Maybe it was a mom-and-pop shop."

"But, then, who was the Spy on my files for the Red Squad?"

"Mr. Berger?" Kevin asks.

"Mrs. Farmer?" I wondered.

"Not Elizabeth," says Kevin. "I saw your files with all the misspellings. She was a spelling-bee queen, remember?"

I stop. "You saw my files?!"

"Didn't you show them to me?"

"Kevin!"

He lied. He kept important information from me. He snooped. We're all through.

"It was I," says Kevin.

"Little George Washington."

I was heartbroken when my love was spurned and now again when it was played with.

I start to sob, noisily, gulpingly.

"You were a holy man," I say. "I loved you for that."

"I've fallen," he says quietly.

"Oh, my ancestors! You were a spy, too?"

It's so hard for me, I can't sit down, yet my legs buckle. He catches me and I hit him.

"No. But Farmer had access to your Red Squad files," he says. "He shows up at Weekend College a few months ago. I don't know why he chose me. Maybe because I was a priest. Nor why he showed them to me. I suspect because I dropped out of the priesthood. He wanted me to know that he knew more about you than I did and that you were, in his words, 'spoiled goods.'"

"And you punched him in the face?"

"No, I learned how one could obtain the files through FOIA. And I wanted you to be aware that he had power over you, that perhaps he could use you—"

We're both silent.

"I can never love you again," I say.

"All right." His shoulders stoop.

"Because you didn't punch him in the face."

We both cry; I loudly, Kevin quietly, the tears running down his cheeks, spotting his tie.

"All those years ago with the Berger," says Kevin, "I got used to being your protector."

Then because we were so sad a minute ago, we laugh hilariously.

"So where was Lobschultz in all this?" I ask, continuing the earlier conversation.

He holds my hand.

"He may have provided the places to meet, his park office, his bookstore. He could have been the public face. And now he can hide in public view."

"He was militarizing the Park Department, I'm sure," I said. "He had a troop of the green elves doing maneuvers at night."

"It may have been fantasyland," said Kevin. "They thought they were taking over."

"They did!" I say.

We stay and visit O'Dwyer every day. We try to get around in Oakland. The Oakland Museum has a startling exhibit, taking me back to the Vietnam War. Oakland was the chief port of departure for the South Pacific and the place of protests. The movement began there!

We drive in the Oakland Hills, that area that was the scene of a devastating fire and is now rebuilt.

And we attend the Oakland East Bay Symphony. Ron was visiting again, and we took in the performance together.

Ron is pleased. "A great African American conductor, and look how he reaches out to the schoolkids in the audience!"

The conductor bows, and the kids give him a standing ovation.

"Maybe they will be standing there one day with a baton!" says Ron, a romantic about the possibilities of overcoming poverty and rising to the top.

I'm studying my Oakland Symphony program.

"I wonder," I said.

Guest pianist, Joseph Stein.

"Give me a minute, will you?" I ask. "I have to go backstage."

The musicians are packing up their instruments. Not the pianist. There he is, silky white shirt, wide white silk tie.

"Little Mozart!" I say.

"Anka, the Greek," he says back to me.

We're quiet. We're both thinking of the same thing, why we stopped playing together.

"Well," says my old neighbor, "I never did go to medical school."

"And I stopped playing Monopoly," I tell him.

What do you say when decades have passed?

"You're still Little Mozart," I say, "and you're also Moe the Most."

"Right," says Joseph. "I play the halls and I play the bars. I swing both ways."

"Ron Ivory is here," I said.

"That's over," he said. "He's too straight for me, straitlaced, that is."

"Did you keep an eye on me in Detroit?"

"Yes," he said. "You were in the hood near Baker's. So, of course, I had to see what was going on with you."

"And?"

"Living alone in a dangerous neighborhood . . . I didn't want harm to come to you."

"That was you walking by?"

"Probably."

"And marking my car?"

"Having a little fun worrying you."

"Trying to get into my apartment?"

"Only once, briefly. I didn't want to get caught in the basement again." He took his leave.

GUEST ARTIST: The poster in front of the Oakland Symphony Hall had a photo of Joseph Stein, KNOWN IN HIS YOUTH AS LITTLE MOZART.

Ron and Kevin were waiting for me impatiently.

It's crisp weather compared with that in the Midwest, with dazzling sun in the afternoon, but it's also freezing mornings and evenings, and no one has central heating.

At night we gather at O'Dwyer's home for the news. Our host is featured daily on TV as a notorious local celebrity. We wait.

Finally, we learn something. A triumphant press conference is coming out of D.C. The press secretary is reassuring the American public that a past terrorist is no longer a danger. That era is over, never to be repeated. O'Dwyer's trial date is being sped up. The press secretary's assistant stands at his side.

"His name is something like J. Edgar Hoover," I say.

"Edgar Miller," says Kevin. "Wasn't he the editor of that right-wing campus press?"

Our pale O'Dwyer leans his head against the couch pillows.

Behind both Lobschultz and Edgar Miller is a familiar figure.

"Former editor of the influential *Park Press*," says Edgar Miller, introducing his aide.

"Mr. Berger!" we shout.

"How did he get the job?" Kevin asks.

"Remember Nixon's press secretary, Ron Ziegler?" O'Dwyer says wearily. "His resume read 'Disneyland.'"

O'Dwyer coughs through the night and, we're told, the following day. His housemates gather their mighty resources, euphemisms for healing the body and spirit. But O'Dwyer continues to breathe noisily.

"Hospitalize him, for God's sake," says Ron, who has been phoned and returns to his friend and former lover. "Take him the fuck in."

The housemates have long distrusted Western medicine.

"Take him in, or I will!" says Ron, who, for a short guy, has a sonorous voice.

Alta Bates Hospital in Berkeley is contacted.

"Tell them to send an ambulance," demands Ron.

"The cost—"

"I'll pay."

When the "ambulette" arrives, so do officers of the law.

"We are monitoring any change," says one.

"To his health?" we ask.

"To his whereabouts," say the officers.

We are confused.

"Everything is a possible ploy," they inform us.

They ride with O'Dwyer in the small ambulette. No room for us. A caravan follows, Pen mates, housemates, and neighbors, the latter wearing T-shirts that read: NEIGHBORS IN HEALTH.

NOW: The Waiting Room

And who is at Alta Bates?

Farmer.

He sees Kevin.

"Regards from Mrs. Farmer," he says.

"You the scum that was just harassing Bernstein in Israel?" I ask.

"That's only the beginning, Miss Anchor," says Farmer.

My name in the files.

"Monitoring all of you. Ever hear of conspiracy?"

"On what?" Kevin asks.

"Aiding and abetting O'Dwyer and his various aliases."

"On what proof?" asks Ron.

"Well, if it isn't the Black Flag exterminator. I mean, the Black Fag," says Farmer. "The proof is looser on conspiracy charges. Remember Benjamin Spock, Mitchell Goodman, et al., and the Boston conspiracy trial during the Vietnam War?"

I do. The others don't.

"I thought you all were so well read," said Farmer. "By your files, at least. That Boston group had never even met one another."

My cell phone rings. I've reset the ring so many times that I don't recognize it at first—Beethoven, Mozart. It keeps ringing.

"Let it go," orders Farmer.

I answer the cell.

"Professor," says a voice. "Don't be concerned."

I turn away from the others.

"Who, who is this?"

"Philip Impelliteri, Doctor," he says politely. "No reason for you to recognize me, but, long ago, you saved my life."

"Philip?" I ask.

Farmer hears and freezes.

"You knew me as Phil," says the deep voice, "Fearless Phil. Now, don't you be afraid. I'm on the case."

"How?" I ask.

Because time is past and present, because most of us are here in this simulated Bullpen, because I'm with the one I so longed for, nothing is expected or unexpected.

"Hang up," says Farmer.

"Stand tough," says Philip. "I'm here to get you all out."

He hangs up. How did he know my number?

"Let me see your cell phone," says Farmer.

I put it in my pocket.

"Of course not, FF," I say.

"FF?" asks Farmer.

"Fuck face."

Kevin blinks at that. "Anka!"

O'Dwyer's doctor comes out for a moment.

"He's in surgery," he says. A pause. "A brain tumor."

"Is it serious?" asks Ron, lips trembling.

"Surgery is always serious," says the attending doctor. "A brain tumor is more serious." He pauses. "It's been growing a long time. There must have been symptoms. Didn't he notice? Didn't he care?"

"Oh, no!" says Ron. "It's shocking!"

The doctor says, "What's shocking is that he didn't attend to it."

"And, miss," he tells me severely, "this gentleman is right," nodding at Farmer. "You're not allowed to use cell phones. Interferes with the machinery." He leaves.

Farmer says, "Well, that could be one of you eliminated."

Ron, once Don Quixote at our Halloween party, stands

threateningly in front of Farmer. Farmer ignores him. Disobeying the doctor, Farmer dials on his own cell. Kevin listens. "Just wondering if it's 313—Detroit—or 245, suburbs," he whispers to me.

There is a rapping on the waiting room window. An attendant shakes his finger at Farmer.

Then this very tall, eccentric-looking man comes into the room. His hair is white. His beard is white. He wears a Greek sailor's cap.

"Hello, Doctor," he says to me. "How are you, Father Kevin?"

THEN: From Comp 101 Onward

Philip had delusions, succeeded by illusions.

He was deluded by justice. Now he's focused on it, all forms of it, abstract justice, the Justice Department, close readings of the rulings of the Supreme Court.

For he had people to focus on—not family, but familylike people, who cared for him, were there at the end of the corridor when he came tramping in. When he hadn't bothered replying to their inquiries, they tracked him down. When he wept, they caught up the tears in soft linen. Despite his absences from the class, he was included in the class anthology, *City Smarts*. Philip was not alone.

He and Boiler Room and Florrie H. took classes together and conferred on homework. One fine holiday Boiler Room O'Connor took him home to meet the "characters," the aunt who worked at Pansy's, the grandmother with the hell or heaven rent parties.

"That's how it is," Father Kevin once told him. "You come out of hell, and you don't go to heaven; you find a middle ground."

"Limbo?" asked Phil.

"Limbo is no longer in favor, along with several saints," said Kevin. "No, it's an in-between space until you find the place just your size."

"'The Three Bears,'" said Phil.

"Exactly," said Kevin. "That's what that fairy tale is all about. Creatures fitting into their very size and place."

"And you?" Phil was bold enough to ask.

"I'm resigning as Father Bear," said Kevin.

It wasn't exactly romanticism, but Phil felt beholden to those Pen mates. Even when they dispersed, when his Big Teacher moved to Ohio and Kevin left the church and the Pen, still Phil held their light inside him and followed it.

NOW

Both the ex-priest and the FBI man recognize him and are surprised.

"You have no reason to either threaten or hold them," says the visitor to Farmer.

"I'm here in an official capacity," says Farmer.

"It's a short step between investigation and harassment," says the white-haired visitor. "You're more officious than official."

It's easy to distract an English teacher with etymology. "Official, officious," I mouth to myself.

"Are you official?" Kevin and I both ask.

"I am," he says.

Too many of us are in the waiting room, although it's clean, with floral silk screens and pleasant intake persons, including orderlies and guards. The guards even bring in chairs if they see you standing for too long. But we are overcrowded: besides the incoming patients, Kevin and me, Ron, housemates, neighbors, and Farmer, who has taken two chairs for himself and his briefcase. And, surprise, Fearless Phil!

"I'm head of the Michigan ACLU," Phil explains, "and on the National Board. I've been monitoring this guy and this case."

So advanced in his career!

Phil says, "There's a point where the personal becomes the retributive."

Retributive!

"That's a very good word, Phil," I say to my A student.

"You know I was always interested in—even obsessed by—justice," says Phil. "These Hoover-era FBI guys went beyond pursuit, into instigation, harassment, and over the boundaries of the law."

"The boundaries have changed, bozo, if you don't know," says Farmer.

Farmer was always sharp tongued; now sarcasm curls his mouth downward. Or is he imitating the facial quirks of the about to be ex-vice president?

"If you make that conspiracy charge," says Phil, "based on propinquity"—Phil winks at me; "propinquity" from a former freshman!—"then you are also a suspect, since, along with the accused, you occupied that same office for those very years."

"I was in the government employ much of that time," says Farmer.

"A stringer?" I ask.

"A freelance undercover guy?" asks Ron.

"A fink?" asks one of O'Dwyer's neighbors. "A singing birdie in our midst!"

"I forgot this is Berkeley." Farmer looks at the neighbor scornfully.

"Oakland!" the neighbor corrects him.

"Actually," says Farmer, "it was my wife who recognized O'Dwyer's photo on the picket line. A little determination, a little magnification!"

"Your wife?" I ask.

"Once and forever," says Farmer.

"Were you guys preparing for war, doing maneuvers in the park?"

"Only some."

"What war?"

"The forever war—the one that doesn't end."

A hospital person opens the door of the waiting room. "Here they are, Mayor," she says.

In walks a pink-shirted man with gold cuff links. He is a buoyant African American, clearly a dignitary.

Philip greets him, "Mayor O'Connor."

The mayor is my age, but something is familiar. When he moves, I remember. My Greystone Ballroom dancing partner!

"Boiler Room!" I exclaim. "Mr. O'Connor!"

"Boiler Room of old," he agrees. "But I left that place a long time ago."

I tell Kevin, "Mr. O'Connor wrote 'Ho in the Sto.'"

"You remember!" says Mr. O'Connor, pleased.

"And 'Heaven and Hell Depression Rent Party,'" I say.

"And you gave me an A on everything, do you remember that?" I do.

"I kept going, Professor," says O'Connor, "on account of you— all through my B.A., got made foreman at the plant."

Philip nods proudly. He's more than kept track of his classmate. They have become close friends.

"Got a call from Solidarity House. The union wanted me to work for them, and on it went."

"It went on to mayor?" I ask.

"I was on a roll after that class," O'Connor says. "School, job, education. Wrote articles for the union paper, wrote speeches for the UAW. Got invited out to Oakland to edit the *Oakland Tribune*. Remember in the bad old days, when William Knowland edited it and it was a right-wing son-of-a-bitch piece of junk, just like the guy who became senator? So, I used the position from the Left, and parlayed editorship into the mayoralty of Oakland."

"Oh, Mr. O'Connor," I say, "this is the best story of all!"

"How did you happen to come to the hospital, Mayor?" Kevin asks.

Our students are the grown-ups, and we are the pupils, awaiting their answers.

"Mr. O'Dwyer is in my constituency," says O'Connor. "His neighbors—these good people—petitioned my office for leniency, saying that he had contributed for years to the community, as a teacher, and you know I'm soft on teachers, and volunteered in community programs. 'He brought health to the community,' they said. A delegation of Neighbors in Health came, and I said I'd look into it. But, before anything could happen, the man took sick."

Farmer said, "We have this under control, Mayor. It's a federal case."

Fearless Phil: "It may not be anybody's case until we hear how he's doing in surgery."

Farmer is not put off. "We got the others."

"What do you think of those tactics, Mayor?" asks Philip. "Haphazard, I'd say. Propinquity is not admission of guilt."

"Philip Impelliteri, Esquire, what else have you got for me," asks O'Connor, "'cause I know you, Philip. You hand in your homework on time."

"I have an affidavit from Arnold Schneider," says Phil, "the chairman of the English department when they all worked there."

"He's still alive?" asks Kevin.

"Alive and in what looked like a pasture for old English profs," says Philip. "He kept me there talking about Swinburne, 'Algernon,'" he imitated. "But still sharp. Remembered them all. He said, 'I was loath to get close to the instructors because their time was finite. After four years they would leave, and it would unsettle me.'"

"He was so unsettled, he fired us," says Kevin.

Philip continues, "He remembered my teacher, Professor Pappas, very well. He said on the night of the bombing she was in his office, paying a social call, as was her occasional wont."

I blush fiercely.

"She was the only young instructor who came in periodically to talk about his specialty. To amuse him, she would bring the latest malapropisms of her students."

"'It was a warm, genital evening,'" say Kevin and Ron.

"We are not amused," says Farmer. "You drove that poor Berger nuts."

"And Dr. Pappas was with him when the bomb went off."

"But it was late," I object. "How could I—"

Philip cuts me off.

"A credible witness testified on your behalf," he says.

Farmer interrupts, "Talking or lap dancing in the old boy's office—the affidavit is of no use. The controls were set on a timer. It could have been anytime, and she could have been doing anything."

"What else, my man?" asks the mayor.

Philip says, "I learned from the chairman the name of his executive secretary. She is also still alive and living alone at home. For obvious reasons, that night was vivid to her. She was staying late in the office going over the Xerox records. 'The young faculty overused the Xerox machine,' she said, 'overused and underpaid. They even put out a magazine, *Moving In*, moving into the office after hours. I thought I might catch them!' she told me.

"She also phoned Father Kevin that very evening to ask him to pay up his share."

"It was for the class!" objected Kevin.

"Father," says Phil.

"Please!" Kevin holds up his hand.

"Professor Kelly," corrects Phil.

"Not yet," says Kevin. "I wasn't a professor then."

Phil pauses when the mayor intervenes.

"I see what you're getting at," says Mayor O'Connor. "Any more?"

"Yes," says Fearless. "I went to see the priest at Jesu Parish, who was acquainted with . . . Mr. Kelly . . . long ago. He vouched for his character, his obedience to the church, and the careful way in which he left it."

Farmer is incensed.

"Obedience to the church? How about a little hootchy-kootchy and taking a toke now and then?"

"Here's where you should be careful," Fearless warns Farmer. "As you remember well, from the O'Dwyer drug case, where there is cannabis at a site all are guilty. From what I have gathered, you supplied the cannabis at your home."

"It was Christmas Eve. A little celebrating," begins Farmer—and then stops.

No wonder he couldn't finish his dissertation. He couldn't think from A to Cannabis!

The mayor shakes his head. "I don't know anything about a drug charge. Is this in addition to the bombing charge?" Mayor O'Connor is looking uncomfortable. "It's a more complicated matter than I thought."

"Mayor," says Philip Impelliteri, "that was a setup, not an unlikely thing to happen in those years."

The mayor agrees. "Setups. Certainly in Oakland with the Black Panthers. Certainly in Chicago with the Fred Hampton murder."

"I even have the name of the retired police officer who 'found' the grass," says Philip. "He boasted of 'sticking it to those guys who were fairies and nigger lovers.'"

The mayor looks serious. "You have that officer's statement?" he asks.

"I do," says Philip. "He was drunk and boastful, but he made it and signed the statement. I had this news for O'Dwyer should he ever reappear, but no chance to tell him. I wanted him to sue."

We are all confused. Too many cases. Too many hard memories. And here is our bald O'Dwyer under the surgeon's knife. Ron Ivory is sitting there on his uncomfortable waiting room chair, boiling. He attacks Farmer.

"What got you?" asks Ron. "You were just a twerp, a country bumpkin, if I recall, who couldn't get his act together. What makes you think you're Jack Webb, a fifties TV remake?"

"Why did you, our only family, become so angry with us?" I ask. "We were so close."

"Even closer than you think," says Farmer. "That Bullpen was claustrophobic. Wherever I went, there you were demonstrating. Whatever I read, there you were letters to the editoring. Secret phone calls, smuggling guys out of the country. Even at the Viet Vet protest, Anka was there, crying with the whiners. When they dropped their medals into the wastebasket, that clanging filled my head. It was too much for me."

When I had seen him at the motel, his head in his hands, he wasn't moved; he was disgusted.

"I went first to the police department and offered my services. They had contacts—Lobschultz, for one. I was offered a freelance contract, investigating radicalism. I couldn't concentrate on classes or students when this betrayal was going on all around me. Even the church betrayed.

"In a way, it started with me. I had been a seminarian, a Benedictine, who had a weakened spirit, quit my studies, and broke my mother's heart. But Kevin, a Jesuit, had been faithful. He had been rewarded for it with his own parish, his adulators. He was powerful because he was not alone. He was one of the sons of the son of God, and he still chose to leave mother church."

Farmer is so strange to us. We had never heard him speak about anything serious. Was it our fault?

He looks at us still angry from forty years ago. "You were just a hodgepodge of people, I decided. Not America."

This time the surgeon comes out, his surgical wear blood-stained.

Quiet in the room. We rise and gather around him.

"Your friend made it through," he says. "But I don't know for how long. The tumor was encapsulated, and I think we got everything. We don't know."

"How should we feel?" asks Ron, choking. "Hopeful, hopeless?"

"Both," says the doctor.

"But if he lives," says Farmer, "he still has to face trial."

"Go home," says the surgeon. "He can't see anyone today. And I know you've been here for hours."

"Jerry taught us how to be healthful," says a churchwoman. "Their house was a co-op, where we got food at bulk prices, fresh produce and fish from the fish market and grains from the supermarkets. He made special arrangements with Trader Joe's and Berkeley Bowl."

Another woman agreed. "He was a saint to us, saving us money, keeping us in good health."

"He made a picket sign for us when we went out on the strike line," said another neighbor. "BAD WAGES ARE UNHEALTHY."

We leave in separate directions: Kevin and I to our motel, O'Connor to the mayor's mansion along with his houseguest, Philip Impelliteri, Esquire. The Neighbors in Health, who had been thinning out as the afternoon wore on, left for their own Oakland homes.

O'Dwyer's housemates are serene. They meditate while they wait. They sit cross-legged, and stretch, doing twisting exercises from their chairs. They are comfortable in their silence.

"He was never exactly one of us," says the aromatherapist, "but he was our light."

"The same with me," says Ron, who leaves with the housemates.

When we get to the motel Kevin and I nap, I tucked under his arm, like a pillow. We awaken at the same time.

"Kevin," I ask, "is this the end of the story?"

"No," says Kevin. "Injustice has to be punished and justice rewarded."

"Not likely," I say. "A fairy tale, my friend. I thought you left all that decades ago."

MOST RECENT: Wrap-up

When we are allowed, we gather, one at a time, at O'Dwyer's bedside. He is somewhat conscious. He recognizes his housemates but not his lover. He recognizes a neighbor but not the Bullpen.

I am getting restless. It's time to return to Ohio. I have dissertations to review. I have my life to discuss.

I open my laptop.

Wait! Wait! It's me, Bernstein! Where are you? I have news! Our old anti-Semite was here and left. I was supposed to be deported. Then it was in limbo.

Then I hear from Mr. Alberg. Remember my student who went to the brothel in Lebanon? He is president of the University of the Negev and vouched for me.

"You were a stimulating teacher," he privately wrote me. "I'm not approving of you or promoting you, just repaying you."

I was told by the government, "Go or stay. It's all the same with us. But, if you stay, behave yourself."

It reminds me of the way Golda used to bawl out her cabinet if they disagreed with her: "Boys, behave yourselves!"

I've been told that O'Dwyer has been found but is ill. He's had enough on his plate, besides sickness. Give him my very best. I didn't much love his poetry but thought he was lovable.

Oh, Bernstein, I thought, always the pedant.

So, dear bullshitters, here's my news. I have the choice—to go home and start over or to stay and continue the fight. I stay!

Get Farmer for me. I should not have been entranced by his fox skull and telephone pole insulators. I thought he was Americana. I guess that's what Americana is—sentimentality and prejudice; carols and curses.

Take care, dear ones. I mean it.

Yaakov

"He's staying!" I weep on Kevin.

"He's right," says Kevin. "It was so important to him to go there, and he has to stay to finish the job."

"But you didn't stay?" I accuse. "You committed yourself to the church and you didn't stay."

"I was right, too," says Kevin.

THEN, JUNE 1969

As my final report I advice [sic] that you keep a beady eye on the suspect, now and in the hereafter.

Past [sic] Script: I appreciate the permission to perform fraternity pranks for freshman initiates: the BB gun and glasses thief. It discombobulated the department and I had a little revenge against those who would C plus me.

BLACKED OUT

NOW

We sit in the waiting room, and I'm reading the *Oakland Tribune*, mostly local information. Neighbors in Health has taken out an ad wishing their beloved Jerry Stewart a speedy recovery and speedy justice. It always takes a minute to remember that was Noble O'Dwyer's alias. He must have hated "Noble." It was not the name by which he called himself or his pen name. Why would his democratic parents name him for the aristocracy? Maybe they named his brother Duke. Where *was* his family? Do they know of his whereabouts? Does he want them to?

My cell rings, and I go out of the waiting room into the admittance room to answer.

"Anka Pappas," I say.

"Hold for His Honor," says a secretarial voice.

"Teacher," I hear. "I want the two of you to meet me at Chez Panisse."

Chez Panisse, where we couldn't even get a rez!

The owner, Alice Waters, greets the mayor warmly.

"How's my queen?" he asks her.

"She's the queen of Berkeley and Oakland," he says, after she's left us. "She wants my kids in Oakland to eat well so she teaches them to grow their own gardens as part of their school program and to eat what they grow! Like my constituent O'Dwyer, or whatever he calls himself, she's into health also."

We order and he turns to me earnestly.

We eat well, our mayor heartier than the rest of us. "Your friend may be a political liability but that could pass. Politics is fluid. Leastwise, I'm willing to take a chance. Tell him he has a place in my administration as Commissioner of Health. After all, we're both Michiganders, even Detroiters, just about family." He stops. "The main thing is, he's got to live."

When we part company the mayor and I reach to embrace. He kisses me smack on the mouth.

"Always wanted to do that!" says the mayor.

Kevin smiles. I'm entitled.

We return to the hospital and to reading the newspapers left around.

"Why does the name Elizabeth Bentley sound familiar?" I ask. "Our Elizabeth, if that's who she is, writes a very reactionary column on the editorial page."

Kevin takes the paper and reads.

"It was Elizabeth Farmer's maiden name," he says. "Remember the spelling-bee winner, Elizabeth Bentley? She's returned to that name. She's named after her great-aunt, she once told me. The aunt was a government witness during the McCarthy era."

"She testified against an all-star cast," I'm remembering. "Alger Hiss and Julius Rosenberg, among about eighty others."

"Yes, Elizabeth Farmer told me," said Kevin.

"Anything else I should know that she told you?"

Kevin looks pained.

I continue, "Elizabeth Bentley was a well-known prevaricator who did much damage. Yet the Bureau used her all the rest of her life."

"She died fairly young, I remember," said Kevin, "and left her niece the royalties on her autobiography."

"And that's when she kicked you out of the house," I said.

"About that time," admits Kevin.

"So, what does all this mean?"

"It means," says Kevin, "that Elizabeth is a columnist for a tabloid and Farmer is about at the end of his time in the FBI."

"How do you know?" I ask.

"Look how jumpy he is. He'll have nothing else to do with the rest of his life."

"Can't we do anything to her, to him?" I ask.

"I don't seem to want to," says Kevin.

"But they can only get more powerful now," I warn him.

"Governments change," says Kevin.

"In the meantime," I plead, "think of the harm they can do."

"Not to me," he says. "Not to us. It's over."

"You're wrong," I tell him. "It's not over. And I'm not rolling over in the clover."

"Why not?" he asks.

"Because I'm a Gray Brigade," I say.

The paper is creased under Bentley's photo. I study the page. "She's still good-looking."

"It's an old photo," he reassures me. "Besides, her kids are in their forties by now!"

"Prickly Holly is forty?"

We sit another moment or two picking up discarded magazines, newspapers.

"Listen to this," says Kevin, laughing. "The president is quoted as saying, 'The trouble with the French is that they don't have a word for *entrepreneur*.'"

We look at each other.

"Mr. Berger!" we say. He was promoted!

FATE: And So It Is Spoken

Our sweet Noble does not awaken. Ron's face is ashy from grief. Against the door of the co-op lies a wreath.

NEIGHBORS IN HEALTH, reads the card.

Fearless Phil is bareheaded, his Greek cap in his hands. "I wanted to tell him the news. My office—the Michigan ACLU— has instituted a suit against the Red Squad and the police department," he says. "The police refuse to give remuneration or to offer an apology, but they'll wipe his record clean." It's unfinished, and that bothers Philip. "I wanted to ask him if I should pursue it further or if the case is settled."

"It's settled," says Kevin.

Ron says, "Do you hear that, Noble, my love? You're clean."

"And with the government?" I ask my A-plus student.

"He'll serve time posthumously," says Fearless Phil.

We prepare to attend the wake of our Pen mate, Noble O'Dwyer.

FATEFUL

My white-robed Fates, begot by Erebus on Night: Clotho, you have spun us; Lachesis, you have measured us and found us of good measure; little Atropos, you have snipped the thread of the one as pale as the clouded moon. Phases of the Moon, Mothers of Fate, we are in your hands.

Kevin is wearing glasses. He pushes them up onto his forehead. He has four eyes, like some mythic creature, one pair smiling, the other blank.

They all regard me.

"You Greeks!" he says.

"I'm Hellenic," I correct.

Kevin is about to make a joke and reconsiders.

We go on with our shared lives.

ACKNOWLEDGMENTS

Deborah Garrison, for bringing devotion and elegance to her work on the novel.

Caroline Zancan and the rest of the editorial staff, in particular Robert Olsson for his inventive page design.

Rebecca Friedman, the ideal agent and critic.

Marcia Freedman, who set me up in Berkeley to begin writing *The Red Squad*.

Carol Jenkins and the Women's Media Center, a nonprofit organization seeking equity for women in the media. Ms. Jenkins provided office space in the Empire State Building so I could complete *The Red Squad*.

Pseudonymous students: "Fearless Phil" and "Florrie H." Phil's poem is rewritten and his future imagined; Florrie H. wrote "A Litany of Names," ending, "This is a love poem / God Didn't Make No Junk."

Marilyn French, Barbara Kane, there, there, always there.

The writer Paul Pines, who drove miles to make me look good.

My husband, the artist Robert Broner, who provided the example.

And our sons and daughters, beloved family.

A NOTE ABOUT THE AUTHOR

E. M. Broner is the author of ten previous books. She has held teaching positions at Wayne State University and Sarah Lawrence College and has been a visiting scholar at Ohio State University, Oberlin College, the University of California at Los Angeles, and Haifa University in Israel. An award-winning playwright and NPR writer, Broner has organized and marched in protests from the time of the Vietnam War up through today and was a pioneer in women's studies and the feminist movement. She was a ritualist, honored by the Wonder Woman Foundation for bringing magic and ritual into the lives of ordinary women. She is also an international speaker and has lectured in Paris, Bordeaux, Jerusalem, Oslo, Copenhagen, and Nairobi. She lives in New York City.

A NOTE ON THE TYPE

The text type in this book was set in Jenson, a font designed for the Adobe Corporation by Robert Slimbach in 1995. Jenson is an interpretation of the famous Venetian type cut in 1469 by the Frenchman Nicolas Jenson (c. 1420–1480).

Composed by North Market Street Graphics, Lancaster, Pennsylvania
Printed and bound by R. R. Donnelley, Harrisonburg, Virginia
Book design by Robert C. Olsson